Here's what teens are saying about Bluford High:

"As soon as I finished one book, I couldn't wait to start the next one. No books have ever made me do that before."
—*Terrance W.*

"The suspense got to be so great I could feel the blood pounding in my ears."
—*Yolanda E.*

"Once I started reading them, I just couldn't stop, not even to go to sleep."
—*Brian M.*

"Great books! I hope they write more."
—*Eric J.*

"When I finished these books, I went back to the beginning and read them all over again. That's how much I loved them."
—*Caren B.*

"I found it very easy to lose myself in these books. They kept my interest from beginning to end and were always realistic. The characters are vivid, and the endings left me in eager anticipation of the next book."
—*Keziah J.*

W9-BXL-798

BLUFORD HIGH

Until We
Meet Again

ANNE SCHRAFF

Series Editor: Paul Langan

SCHOLASTIC INC.
New York Toronto London Auckland Sydney
Mexico City New Delhi Hong Kong Buenos Aires

If you purchased this book without a cover,
you should be aware that this book is stolen property.
It was reported as "unsold and destroyed" to the publisher,
and neither the author nor the publisher has received
any payment for this "stripped book."

No part of this publication may be reproduced,
stored in a retrieval system, or transmitted in any form
or by any means, electronic, mechanical, photocopying,
recording, or otherwise, without written permission of the publisher.
For information regarding permission, write to Townsend Press, Inc.,
1038 Industrial Drive, West Berlin, NJ 08091.
Visit Townsend Press on the Web at
www.townsendpress.com.

ISBN-13: 978-0-439-90488-9
ISBN-10: 0-439-90488-9

Copyright © 2002 by Townsend Press, Inc.
All rights reserved. Published by Scholastic Inc.,
557 Broadway, New York, NY 10012, by arrangement
with Townsend Press, Inc. SCHOLASTIC and associated logos
are trademarks and/or registered trademarks of Scholastic Inc.

12 11 10 9 8 7 6 5 4 3 2   7 8 9 10 11 12/0

Printed in the U.S.A.   01

First Scholastic printing, September 2007

Chapter 1

"Girls, sit down. Your father and I have something important to tell you."

Darcy Wills glanced at her sister Jamee, wondering if she knew what their mother was about to announce. Jamee, fourteen years old and two years younger than Darcy, shrugged her shoulders and sat down at the table.

"We've been doing a lot of thinking lately," Mom said nervously, sitting down at the head of the table. Darcy's father sat beside her, gently holding her hand. "We've decided to give our marriage a second chance."

Darcy's heart jumped into her throat, and Jamee nearly fell out of her chair.

"For real!" Jamee cheered, putting her hands on either side of her face as if she could barely believe what she just heard.

"That's right," her father added. "We've been going to counseling and we're gonna try and make it work, for us, for you two, and for Grandma." Dad's eyes glistened as he spoke, and Darcy knew he meant every word.

Only months ago, he had reappeared after a five-year absence. Darcy was just eleven years old when he abandoned the family. For years, she had made up stories to explain why he had left. But later, when she found out that he had taken off with another woman, Darcy decided she would never forgive him for the hurt he caused.

Then, last fall, he came back like a stranger one evening. Since that time, he did everything he could to help Darcy, Jamee, and their mother. He even admitted his mistakes, apologized to each of them, and swore to be a father again. At first, Darcy did not believe him, but months had passed, and he was still there, offering advice, support, and love. And now this.

"Girls, I understand this might be difficult. I'm not going to forget what your father did, and I don't expect you to either," Mom added, looking at her husband. "But he's a different man now. I believe what he says, and we both want us to be a family again."

Before Mom finished her sentence, Jamee got up and hugged her parents. "I'm so happy," she repeated over and over again.

Darcy quickly followed, putting her arms around her parents. The years of bitterness seemed to thaw in the embrace. Even though part of her was still angry at her father, another bigger part was thrilled that he was back and that he wanted to be with them.

"There's something else we want to tell you," Mom said, gently pulling away from the hug. "We're moving."

"What?" Darcy yelled, pretending to be surprised. Her father had admitted to Jamee and Darcy that he wanted to move the family out of their old apartment and into a nearby house. He had even taken Darcy and her sister to see the house, though he never promised them he would buy it.

"We found a small house a few blocks away. It's so close you two will still able to go to Bluford High School, but it has more room and a nice little yard for Grandma," Mom explained. "We'll be moving in about a week."

"I can't believe this. Wait till I tell everyone at school!" Jamee said with a wide toothy smile. Darcy agreed. She couldn't wait to tell her friends about the sudden changes in her life.

As she got ready for bed that night, Darcy wondered if there were any other surprises in store for her in the days ahead.

The next morning, Darcy raced off to Bluford High, eager to tell her boyfriend Hakeem the good news about her family. Over the past year, Darcy and Hakeem had become very close. Months ago, he helped her deal with the sudden arrival of her father and was supportive weeks later when Jamee ran away from home. Darcy got even closer to Hakeem when he told her his father had been diagnosed with cancer earlier in the year. At least now, Darcy figured, she had something good to share with him. As she reached school, Darcy spotted Hakeem riding his silver motorbike into the school parking lot.

"Hakeem!" she cried, running over to him. "I've got the best news! My parents are getting back together, and we're moving into a new house with a back-yard and everything!"

Hakeem gave Darcy a hug, but she felt right away that there was something wrong. His arms were like dead weights around her, and the embrace did not last long before Hakeem pulled away.

"That's great, Darcy," he said, getting off the motorbike. He began to walk ahead, shoulders down and staring at the ground. Darcy remained a few steps behind, stunned.

"Hakeem, is everything okay?"

Hakeem stopped and slowly turned to look at her. "D-dad c-can't handle the job like he used to," said Hakeem, stuttering as he often did when nervous, "not since the chemotherapy t-treatments. That cancer really whipped him bad. He works two or three hours, then he's no good for the rest of the day."

Darcy walked up to Hakeem and took his hand. "I'm sorry, Hakeem," she said, suddenly feeling foolish.

"It's not good," Hakeem continued, shaking his head. "Dad's brother has a store in Detroit, where they sell furniture and TV's and stuff, and he's offered Dad a job there. It would be a lot easier for him to handle, mostly keeping up with the inventory. Dad's real good with numbers. He just can't work real long hours, that's all."

Darcy felt as if her heart had dropped into her knees. *Detroit?* It was so far from California, it might as well be another planet. For a second, Darcy's tongue felt glued to the back of her throat, and she was unable to speak.

"So does this mean you're going to move?" she asked.

"Yeah, if Dad takes the job," Hakeem said somberly. "He hasn't made up his mind yet. He said he needs to talk to his doctors. But if he decides to take it, we would leave as soon as the school year ends."

Darcy's mind spun like a whirlwind. Waking up this morning, Darcy felt as if her life was on a wonderful upswing, and nothing could go wrong. Now everything felt different. Just as quickly as she had gotten her family back, Darcy was now at risk of losing her boyfriend.

"I . . . I don't know what to say," Darcy stammered, forcing back tears.

"Nothing is definite yet," Hakeem assured her. "I just wanted you to know that I might have to move away."

Hakeem's last words seemed to hang in the air. *Move away.* Just minutes earlier she had so many plans for the summer. Now all that was threatened.

"You can't leave Bluford now," she declared. "I mean, don't you have a relative or someone you could live with? Maybe you could stay with Cooper or something." Cooper Hodden was one of Hakeem and Darcy's closest friends. She was sure Cooper would let Hakeem stay with his family. Even as she spoke, Darcy knew she was being selfish, but she could not stop herself. She felt as if someone was robbing her.

"I can't leave my family, Darcy. They depend on me," Hakeem said, stepping away from her, as if something she said pained him. "Look, I don't know how this is all gonna turn out. The doctors don't even know, not yet. But if Mom and Dad and the rest of the kids have to go to Detroit, then I have to be there, too. I don't want to go, but—"

The school bell rang loudly, signaling the start of morning classes. "We gotta go, Darcy. We'll talk about this later." Hakeem quickly turned and rushed into the building, leaving Darcy alone in the parking lot.

Tarah Carson, Darcy's closest friend, shook her head when Darcy told her Hakeem might be moving. They were standing at a water fountain between classes. "Girl," Tarah said, "Hakeem's father is real sick. That chemo is tough to handle. I know because my neighbor went through it, and he ain't been himself ever since."

"But what about *us*?" Darcy wailed. "This was supposed to be our first summer together."

"Listen, Darcy. Right now Hakeem's gotta do what he can for his family. They're all goin' through this, not just him. His little sisters and his mother are sufferin' too," Tarah explained.

"I know what you're saying, and I feel bad for them, especially for his dad," Darcy said, wiping her eyes. "But at the same time, I feel so bad for me, too. Is that wrong, Tarah? Am I a bad person to feel that way?"

"No, Hakeem's your boyfriend. Of course you don't want to see him go! If someone told me Cooper had to move, I don't know what I'd do," she admitted, giving Darcy a sympathetic hug. "But you gotta put yourself in his shoes too."

Darcy nodded. "Thanks, Tarah," she said, fighting back more tears. She knew Tarah was right. Moving would be harder on Hakeem than anyone else. Besides worrying about his father, he would be losing everything—his school, his friends, his neighborhood, and her. But understanding Hakeem's troubles only made her feel worse. *What about us?* she thought to herself again, dread gathering in her chest like storm clouds in a summer sky.

After school, Darcy went straight home. She wasn't in the mood to talk to anyone. Normally, she would go into her bedroom when she wanted to be alone, but now her room was cluttered with boxes in preparation for moving into the new house. Frustrated, she sat in the living room and flipped through a magazine. Jamee arrived from school a few minutes later.

"Hey, Darcy, guess what?" Jamee said, throwing her school bag on the couch. "Liselle Mason, the girl who lives across the street, wants to hire you."

"Hire me? For what?" Darcy asked. "I hardly know her." Liselle had been a junior at Bluford when Darcy was in eighth grade. All Darcy remembered about Liselle was that she had been popular until she got pregnant and dropped out of Bluford. Once in a while, Darcy saw Liselle at the grocery store, but she never said more than a quick hello.

"I ran into her outside, and she told me she needs a babysitter. She asked me if you were available," Jamee said, fishing a piece of paper from her pocket. "She needs someone to watch her baby while she goes back to school. Here's her phone number. I told her you'd call her."

Darcy was surprised by Liselle's offer. Still, she could use the money. And working would be better than sitting around feeling sorry for herself if Hakeem left, she thought. "Thanks. I'll call her tonight," Darcy said, getting up from the couch to check on Grandma.

In the darkened bedroom, Darcy found Grandma sitting in her chair staring into space.

"Hey, Grandma," Darcy said, kneeling down and taking her grandmother's thickly-veined hand. "We're gonna move into our new house soon. That'll be so good. We're gonna have a backyard and you can watch the birds—"

"I'm cold," Grandma declared, even though it was warm in the apartment. "Why isn't the heater on?"

"I'll get your shawl, Grandma," Darcy said. She went to the nearby dresser and reached into the top drawer.

"Is that better?" she asked, draping the shawl on Grandma's thin shoulders.

"No," she snapped. "It's still cold."

Darcy noticed that her grandmother seemed to be having more cranky spells lately. *Could her condition be worsening?* Darcy wondered. Ever since Grandma's first stroke over a year ago, Darcy feared that the family might be forced to send Grandma to a nursing home. She imagined her grandmother calling out her name in the middle of the night, only to have a stranger appear at her bedside. The thought of Grandma alone and frightened in unfamiliar surroundings made Darcy shudder. There was no way she would allow Grandma to be put into such a place. No way.

After dinner, Darcy called Liselle Mason. "Thanks for calling," Liselle said. "I guess your sister told you why I asked you to call."

"Yes," Darcy replied. "She said you were looking for a babysitter."

"That's right. I'm heading back to school this summer, and I wanted to know if you'd be interested in babysitting my daughter a couple days a week. She's just two years old, but she's an angel."

"I'd love to watch her for you," Darcy said, trying to sound enthusiastic, though her thoughts kept drifting back to Hakeem. Darcy agreed to visit Liselle's apartment and meet the baby after school the next day. As soon as she hung up the phone with Liselle, Darcy tried to call Hakeem, but his phone was busy. She gave up after two more attempts.

Why doesn't he call me? she wondered as she lay in bed that night. Her small bedroom was almost completely packed and ready to be moved. In the darkness, the shadows of boxes and the stale smell of cardboard made her room seem eerie and unfamiliar. Everything she had grown used to seemed to be changing. Some of it was good, and some was bad. But it was all different, and Darcy felt powerless to stop it.

"I wish some things never changed," Darcy whispered, thinking of Hakeem and wondering why he didn't call.

Chapter 2

Darcy did not see Hakeem at Bluford the next day. Though she worried about him, she had to leave right after school to meet Liselle Mason.

Liselle lived across the street from the Willses' old apartment, though her building was a bit more rundown than theirs. Patches of graffiti dotted some portions of the building's exterior, and rusting iron bars covered the windows on the first two floors. Inside, the hallways seemed clean, though, and Darcy noticed nothing seemed to be falling apart.

"I'm coming," said a friendly voice when Darcy knocked on the door. The door opened seconds later. Darcy knew immediately it was Liselle. She looked older and a bit heavier than the girl Darcy remembered, but her eyes were the same. When Darcy was in eighth grade, Liselle always seemed to be hanging out of some boy's car window, cursing loudly and laughing. Now she looked like a woman, not a girl.

"Well look at you!" Liselle exclaimed, glancing up and down at Darcy. "You certainly have grown since we were in school together. I bet you got all the boys' heads turning."

"Not really," Darcy said, a bit embarrassed by Liselle's attention. "Thanks for offering me this job," Darcy added, hoping to change the subject.

"Darcy, I'm just glad you're available," Liselle confessed. "You know how hard it is to find a good babysitter? I know you'll be good. I remember how you were in school, always gettin' the grades and bein' responsible and mature," Liselle continued. "Even when you were in middle school, I could tell that you were that way. Other kids may have made fun of you, but where are they now? I'd never trust my baby with any of the people I was friends with back in high school, but I know I can trust you."

"Thanks," Darcy replied, unsure if she should feel flattered or a little insulted.

Just then, a chubby toddler emerged from the bedroom and ran into Liselle's knees. "Kelena, I want you to meet somebody," Liselle said tenderly, picking up the toddler and handing her to Darcy. "Say hello to Darcy, baby." Kelena put her hand in her mouth and stared into Darcy's eyes. Her soft round face looked just like her mother's. Darcy instantly fell in love with the baby.

"She's beautiful!" Darcy exclaimed, lifting Kelena high into the air. "I would love to take care of her, Liselle."

"She's my pride and joy," Liselle said, beaming. "Now you see why I got to get back to school. She deserves better than this place. I can't wait to get a good job so I can afford my own apartment and won't have to share it with no one, especially Brian. I may love him cause he's my brother, but that don't mean I always got to like him."

Darcy had not heard anything about Brian Mason for years. She remembered that he was a year older than Liselle and that he had gone to nearby Lincoln High School where he played football. Darcy had heard rumors that he was kicked out of school for something, but she never knew what happened. Until now, she had no idea that he had been living with Liselle.

"But I should stop complainin'," Liselle continued. "If it wasn't for the money he's making at his security job, I wouldn't be able to live here or go to school," she said thoughtfully. "Besides, he works so much he's hardly ever here. You probably won't even see—"

Just then, the front door of the apartment opened, and a young man wearing a navy-blue uniform rushed into the living room. He was tall and broad-shouldered with cinnamon-colored skin and close-cropped hair. "I forgot my beeper and I . . . ," he explained but then stopped when he saw Darcy.

"Well, speak of the devil," Liselle said. "We were just talking about you. Darcy, this is my brother, Brian."

Brian stepped toward Darcy with his arm extended. "Don't believe anything my sister says about me," he said, gently but firmly shaking Darcy's hand. His eyes were intense, and she noticed he had a wide mouth with perfect white teeth which contrasted nicely with his dark skin.

"Nice to meet you," Darcy replied, noticing he wore a musky cologne.

"Darcy will be babysitting for me after school, Brian," Liselle explained. "And I already told her all about you, so

16

don't you be gettin' on her nerves when I ain't here."

"Don't worry. I'm not going to bother her at all," Brian said, giving Darcy a playful smirk. "I just came home to get my beeper. The boss likes me to have it all the time, just in case he needs to reach me." For an instant, he stared at Darcy and smiled. She could feel herself beginning to blush under his intense gaze. At one point, Brian seemed to nod slightly as he looked at her. Then he grabbed the beeper off the coffee table and turned toward the door.

"Well, I guess I'll see you around then," Brian said with a grin. He glanced one last time at Darcy before walking out the door.

Darcy smiled. "He seems nice," she said to Liselle after Brian left.

"Oh, he's real smooth all right. Don't let him fool you," Liselle said, rolling her eyes.

On her way home, Darcy wondered about Brian and why Liselle seemed so bothered by him, but then her thoughts turned to Hakeem. She hoped that she would speak to him soon and he would tell her that the move to Detroit had been canceled. As she waited to cross

17

the street, Darcy saw Tarah and her boyfriend, Cooper Hodden, heading in her direction.

"Girl, you look like a zombie walking around in a daze," Tarah said.

"I just got a lot on my mind," Darcy replied.

"I betcha I know what you were thinking about," Cooper said, smiling. "Or should I say, *who* you were thinking about."

"Shut up, Coop," Tarah scolded, playfully hitting him on his chest. "Hakeem leaving is bad enough without you makin' a big fuss about it."

Darcy cringed. "It isn't even definite that Hakeem is moving away. His father has some really good doctors, and maybe they'll make him healthy again."

"Don't bet on it," Cooper said. "Things usually don't go the way we want them to. I always plan for the worst. Then if I'm wrong, at least I'm gettin' good news. That's what you should do. Plan for Hakeem to move to Detroit at the end of the school year, and expect that you'll never see him again."

"Thanks a lot, Coop," Darcy said sarcastically. "That makes me feel so much better."

Tarah gave Cooper a swift nudge in the ribs. "Will you just keep your mouth shut?"

"Why?" Cooper asked. "I'm only bein' realistic."

"No, you're bein' stupid," Tarah snapped. "Look Darcy, even if Hakeem moves away, which I hope he doesn't, you two can still keep in touch."

"I wonder what the girls are like in Detroit," Cooper blurted out.

Darcy and Tarah both glared at him angrily.

"Come on," Cooper said, "I'm just kidding. Darcy, you know Hakeem's got his eyes only on you."

"Yeah, Darcy," Tarah said, "Hakeem ain't lookin' at nobody else."

"Look, guys. I gotta get home. I'll talk to you later," Darcy said. She turned and headed across the street. She was not in the mood for either of them. Cooper's jokes hurt her, and Tarah's words only made her more worried.

If Hakeem left, would they keep in touch as Tarah said? Darcy wondered. Hakeem barely even called her now, and he lived only a few blocks away. What would happen if he moved to a new city? And what about the girls he would meet in Detroit? Darcy knew that as soon as

Hakeem pulled out his guitar and began singing, they would flock to him just as they did at Bluford.

Maybe it's just a matter of time, Darcy thought, *until I completely vanish from his mind.*

On Saturday, Darcy and her family moved into their new house. While it was only three blocks from their old apartment, it seemed like an entirely new neighborhood. Instead of directly bordering the sidewalk, the house had a patch of grass in front of it the size of a compact car. There was even a tiny fenced-in backyard with a small cement patio, a young tree and a few bushes.

Up until the day before the move, Darcy's mother appeared quite calm. But on moving day when she and Dad took their belongings to the house, Mom's demeanor changed completely.

"My goodness! What a beautiful room," Mom exclaimed when she first saw the master bedroom. "Look how big. Oh my!" she gasped over and over again.

"Remember, Mattie, I promised you a room fit for a queen," Dad said proudly. "Well, here it is. I'm finally making good on my promises."

Darcy was thrilled to see her mother overwhelmed with joy in the center of the spacious room. "Carl, I can't believe my eyes. I feel like pinchin' myself, just to make sure I'm not dreamin'," Mom said happily. "This is really our home?"

"Mattie, you and the girls deserve this and more," Dad said, hugging her.

The family was making a new start, Darcy thought. Everyone seemed ready to put the painful past behind them, almost as if it had never happened. Even Jamee was caught up in the excitement of the move, going from room to room saying, "Can you believe this?"

Darcy wanted to feel as enthusiastic as the rest of her family, but she could not. Where everyone else focused on the family's new beginning, Darcy kept worrying about what might be ending. Standing in her new house, Darcy could not stop thinking about Hakeem moving to Detroit.

"Angelcake, what's happening?" Grandma asked, snapping Darcy out of her thoughts. In the new living room, surrounded by unfamiliar walls and furniture, Grandma looked uncomfortable and small in her wheelchair.

"We're in our new house, Grandma," Darcy said. Then she gently wheeled the frail woman from room to room and explained what each room was.

"Look, Grandma," Darcy said, moving her outside to the tiny patio in the backyard, "in that tree there's a birdhouse, and it's already full of birds." Darcy was happy to see that the tree provided shade and blocked some of the view of the surrounding houses and apartment buildings.

"Are the birds singing?" Grandma asked, gently tilting her head to see the clusters of birds perched in the tree's branches. A thin smile stretched over her weathered face.

"Yes," Darcy said, kneeling beside the wheelchair. It warmed her heart to see Grandma happy. Darcy had worried about whether Grandma would be able to handle the stress of living in a new home. Seeing Grandma smile made Darcy feel the new house might actually improve Grandma's health.

"I like to hear the birds sing," Grandma said. "I want to hear them sing to me every day." She lifted her frail hand and waved to the birds.

Just then, Jamee stepped outside. She gave Grandma a hug and said, "Isn't this great? Aren't we all so lucky?"

"Blessed," Grandma smiled. "We are all blessed. I'm so glad we moved back to Alabama. It's good to be home."

Darcy and Jamee exchanged a sad look. Grandma had not been the same since her stroke. The once-powerful, strong-willed woman was now a shadow of her former self.

"I'm tired, Angelcake. I'm tired," Grandma said softly after a few minutes outside. Darcy quickly helped Grandma into bed for a nap. Leaving the old woman's bedroom, Darcy walked through the new house, listening to the sounds of her family getting settled. Jamee kept running back and forth to the car to unload her belongings. Mom and Dad were talking softly, their conversation occasionally interrupted by Dad's booming laughter. At times, Darcy could hear Mom let out a nervous giggle, as if she was suddenly happy, but afraid to admit it.

Darcy wondered if they would be okay in the new house. It seemed like only yesterday when Dad ran out on the family, and Mom was forced to move into their old apartment, with its small rooms and cracked ceiling. Darcy remembered how much her mother cried and how

Grandma held Mom in her arms like a little girl. Darcy had been in elementary school at the time, but the sight of her mother in that state still haunted her.

Looking at the bright carpet and freshly painted walls of their new house, Darcy hoped there were no more shocks in their future. But with her thoughts drifting uneasily to Hakeem and Grandma, Darcy had her doubts.

Hakeem was absent from school again Monday. He had called Darcy to explain he would be with his father at the hospital. The doctors were checking to see if the cancer was in remission. Darcy worried all day and was anxious to call Hakeem after school.

As soon as her final class ended, Darcy bolted out of Bluford. Outside, heat from the blazing June sun made the asphalt beneath her feet soft and sticky. Stopping to wait for a traffic light, Darcy heard the approaching rumble of rap music being pumped through a powerful stereo system. She glanced toward the sound and noticed a car full of unfamiliar boys. They seemed to be her age, and they were staring at her.

"Hey, girl. You need a ride? I got

room for you right here," said the boy in the passenger seat, gesturing for her to get inside.

"Or you could come back here with me," another called out from the back seat. The driver laughed wildly.

"No thanks," Darcy said, glad to see the light turn green.

"Oh, she think she special or somethin'," another boy added. Turning up the music even louder, the boys slowly drove off.

Darcy quickly crossed the street and approached her old apartment building. As she passed her former home, Darcy noticed a shiny red Toyota Camry parked across the street in front of Liselle's. "Hey Darcy," a familiar voice called out. "What a coincidence." Brian emerged from the car holding a cloth.

"What are you doing here, Brian?" she asked.

"I was just cleanin' my car," he explained, flashing a wide white smile. "Now it's my turn. What are you doin' here? My sister said you moved."

"We did. My house is only a few blocks up the street."

"Can I give you a ride home?" he asked.

Darcy hesitated for a moment. Brian was wearing a white T-shirt, which showed off thick cords of muscles on his arms and shoulders. He was handsome too. There was only a short walk left, but she had no reason not to accept a ride from Brian. Besides, she did not want to be hassled by the boys again.

"Sure," Darcy said, crossing the street. "Thanks." She climbed into the car. It was spotless and had dark tinted windows and a miniature gold and red crown mounted on the dashboard.

"That's my crown," Brian said proudly. "I'm the king of this castle on wheels. Still lookin' for my queen."

"It's a really nice car. I can't wait until I get a car of my own. Then I could go anywhere," Darcy said, imagining herself driving to see Hakeem in Detroit.

"Well consider me at your service, Darcy. Whenever you need a lift, just let me know," Brian offered as he pulled away from the curb. "I'll get you where you need to go."

"Thanks," Darcy said, wondering if he was serious.

"Liselle really digs you," he said, changing the subject. "She's glad you're keepin' an eye on Kelena while she's at school."

"I like Liselle a lot." Darcy smiled. "Kelena too." As she spoke, Brian stopped the car at a red light, and a small object rolled out from under the seat and bumped Darcy's shoe. It was a chocolate-colored lipstick tube. Brian did not seem to notice it, so Darcy nudged it back under the seat.

"So, you a sophomore at Bluford?" he asked.

"Yeah, but only for a few more days," Darcy answered. "I can't believe I'll be a junior next year. Some days it seems like I just started at Bluford. Other days it seems like I've been there forever."

"I know what you mean," Brian nodded. "It only gets worse as you get older. Trust me."

Darcy smiled and looked out the window.

"You know, you seem more mature than any high-school girl I know," he added.

"Thanks," Darcy said, flattered. "Not everybody feels that way about me. Oh, that's it. That's our new place." She pointed to her family's new house.

"It looks great," he said as he pulled up in front of the house. "I guess now I know where to find you."

"I appreciate the ride," Darcy said, getting out of the car. "Thanks again."

"Ain't no big thing. Besides, you got plenty of time to thank me now that you're working for my sister," he said, raising an eyebrow.

As the Camry slowly pulled away, Darcy found herself smiling and waving, pleased with Brian's interest. But as he vanished around the corner, she thought of Hakeem and rushed up the front walkway. It was Hakeem she wanted to be with. It was Hakeem she needed to speak to.

Chapter 3

"Hey sweetheart," Dad called out when Darcy came home. He was still dressed in the dark suit he wore to his job at an upscale men's clothing store. "Mom just left for work. Another nurse called out sick, so she's got a double shift tonight. I told her to say no, but you know your mother."

Darcy smiled. She knew Dad wanted to be the family provider. It bothered him that Mom worked so much. Yet she also knew her mother was not about to depend on Dad's money, not after what he had done. She remembered what Mom said five years ago after Dad ran out on the family—*"I ain't ever gonna depend on a man again."* When Dad left, Mom sometimes worked sixty hours a week to take care of Darcy, Jamee, and Grandma and to pay the rent. If it had not been for

Mom's nursing job, the whole family would have been penniless. But Darcy knew that mentioning how important Mom's income had been would only hurt Dad's feelings.

"How's Grandma?" she asked, noticing the empty wheelchair in the living room.

"She's fine," Dad said. "We were singing old church hymns a little while ago. Your grandma don't sing much no more, but she likes to clap her hands. We had a good time, but she's resting now."

Darcy went to the kitchen and grabbed the telephone. She quickly dialed Hakeem's number. After a few rings, Hakeem answered "Yeah?" with an unusual edge to his voice.

"Hakeem, it's me. I just wanted to know how your dad was . . . I mean, how were the tests?" Darcy asked.

"We didn't get any results yet. That's how this stuff is. It takes a while. But I got things to do 'round here, and I'm waiting for a call from my uncle. Can't we just talk tomorrow?" Hakeem asked.

"Yeah, I guess," Darcy replied, stunned at how abrupt Hakeem was. A second later she heard a click, and Hakeem was gone. She hung up the phone and leaned against the wall.

Hakeem has never treated me so rudely, Darcy thought. She knew he was under a lot of stress, but usually he talked to her, or at least tried to. She wanted to reach out to Hakeem, but she did not know how, not this time.

Frustrated, Darcy trudged into the living room and collapsed on the chair next to her father.

"What's botherin' you, baby?" he asked.

"Nothing," Darcy grumbled, trying to hide her feelings.

"Come on, Darcy," Dad said. "I know something heavy's on your mind. What is it?"

Darcy took a deep breath. "It's Hakeem," she admitted. "His dad is very sick, and now he might move to Detroit with the family. I might never see him again."

Her father nodded thoughtfully as she spoke. When she finished, he folded his arms on his chest and looked up as if he were searching for something in the ceiling. "Well now," he began, shifting his body several times. "That's a tough one. I'm no expert on high school romances," he continued cautiously, appearing uneasy, "but I know most guys and girls

31

usually don't stick with the people they date in high school. You're gonna like lots of guys before you find the right one. Hakeem's a nice guy, but you'll meet others. Give it some time. You haven't even gotten to college yet."

Darcy rolled her eyes at her father's words. How dare he suggest her relationship with Hakeem was trivial? "Dad, I don't want anyone else!" she yelled, struggling to calm herself. "I really care about Hakeem. Can't you understand that?"

"I'm sorry, baby," Dad said, lowering his head.

"It's okay," Darcy said, getting up. She went to her bedroom, closed the door, and flopped down on her bed. A stack of boxes from the old apartment still sat in a corner of the room, but she did not feel like unpacking them. She knew they contained relics of the past— pictures, a few posters, stuffed animals, and some books. Looking through them now would just make her feel depressed, and she already felt sad enough.

Darcy could not shake being bothered by what her father said. Part of her wished she had not told him anything. But another part wondered if Dad's words might be true.

Arriving at school the next morning, Darcy saw Hakeem pull his motorbike into the parking lot. She hurried over to him. "Hi," she said, trying to sound upbeat. "What's up?"

"Hey," Hakeem grunted, barely looking at her. "Dad is pretty sure that we'll be leaving, Darcy," he said, in a somber voice. "The doctors say it'll be a while before he regains his strength, and my uncle has promised him a good job, so Dad says we gotta go."

Darcy felt her legs buckle, as if someone had pulled a trap door out from under her. "So . . . when will you be leaving?" she stammered, steadying herself, her heart pounding heavily.

"School gets out on June tenth. We'd leave right after that, so it'll be in two weeks." With those words, Hakeem turned away.

"So soon? I didn't think things would happen so fast," Darcy said. She knew tears were welling up in her eyes, but she did not care. She wanted Hakeem to see how much he meant to her, how devastated she was. Tears rolled down both sides of her face.

"Aren't you even upset?" Darcy challenged, angered by how unemotional he seemed. "This could mean the end for us!"

"Look, Darcy, don't make this any harder," Hakeem replied, finally turning around. "I don't like it any more than you do." Then he slung his backpack over his shoulder and headed toward Bluford. Darcy wanted him to say something else, something more, but he was silent. She felt cheated, as if events were conspiring to make her life miserable.

"Hakeem, wait!" Darcy cried. "There must be something you can do to stay." She hurried behind him as he spoke.

"Darcy, just drop it!" he snapped, turning back to her. Darcy noticed for the first time that his eyes were puffy and red. "I'm moving to Detroit, and that's it. There's nothing anybody can do about it." Hakeem stormed off, leaving her standing alone in the parking lot. Through a blur of tears, Darcy watched him climb the steps into Bluford and vanish inside, without looking back.

At lunchtime, Darcy sobbed on Tarah's shoulder. "He's leaving right after school's out, and he doesn't even care!"

"Of course he does, girl," Tarah comforted her. "Why else did he get so angry? You think he wants to leave all his friends behind and not be here to finish high school? He's leaving *everything*, not just you."

"But we had everything all planned out," Darcy explained. "We were going to go to the junior and senior proms together. And we'd all graduate together in two years and—"

"Darcy, I'm sure Hakeem wanted to do those things too," Tarah interjected.

"But, he won't even talk to me," Darcy said. "I feel like we used to be so close, but not anymore. Now he's just shut me out completely."

"Darcy, that boy's whole family is in all kinds of turmoil, you hear what I'm sayin'? And Hakeem's got to think of his family first. It's only right," Tarah said. "He's been your boyfriend for a few months, but he's been in that family for seventeen years."

Before Darcy could reply, she noticed Brisana Meeks approaching the lunch table.

"Oh great, here comes Brisana," Darcy mumbled. The last thing she wanted to do was talk to her. Only a year ago, Darcy would have looked forward to seeing Brisana. But ever since Darcy had befriended Cooper and Tarah, Brisana had become rude. Darcy had spoken to Brisana about her attitude, and it helped. But whenever Brisana saw Darcy with Tarah or Cooper, she still seemed bitter and hostile. To make matters worse, Tarah did not have much patience for Brisana. Each time the two girls got near each other, there was an uncomfortable tension between them. As Brisana got closer to the table, Darcy braced herself, hoping that Tarah and Brisana would be civil to each other.

"Hi, Darcy," Brisana said, ignoring Tarah. "I hear Hakeem is leaving Bluford. You must be upset. But not too upset," she added with a smile.

"What are you trying to say, Brisana?" Darcy asked.

"I saw you riding around with Brian Mason yesterday, so I figure you are bouncing back from Hakeem, real quick," she replied snidely.

Oh no, she's starting trouble again, Darcy thought. "Listen, Brisana, I'm just babysitting for his sister Liselle after school," Darcy explained. "He gave me a ride home. That's all."

"Darcy, you don't have to explain nothin' to her," Tarah said, turning to

Brisana. "Girl, this ain't any of your business, and if you don't have anything else to say, then I suggest you get steppin' right now." Tarah added, rolling her neck, with her hands on her hips.

"Anyway," Brisana said, frowning and turning back to Darcy. "I just thought you should know the kind of guy you're running around with."

"I'm not running around with anyone, Brisana," Darcy snapped. "All he did is give me a ride home because he was being nice. There's no law against that."

"Trust me, Darcy," Brisana replied, "it's an act. Brian Mason's only nice to girls because he wants one thing. You better stay away from him or you're going to run into trouble. Believe me, I know."

"Girl, don't you be tryin' to make trouble," Tarah said, standing up. "You heard what Darcy said. He was just bein' nice. So you need to mind your own business, like I told you before. Goodbye."

Brisana turned and stormed away without a word.

"See," Tarah said loud enough for Brisana to hear. "That's how you have to handle her, girl. She's like those flies that try to ruin cookouts. You just gotta swat 'em away."

Darcy got up shaking her head. She could not be bothered worrying about what Brisana said. Her mind was still on Hakeem. As she emptied her lunch tray, she wondered what would happen in the months to come.

"I hope you don't stop livin' 'cause of all this," Tarah said, interrupting Darcy's thoughts.

"What do you mean?"

"I mean, I hope you don't turn your life off once Hakeem leaves. You can still have fun, girl."

"No, I can't," Darcy said softly, her voice beginning to crack. "This ruins everything, especially the summer. I wanted us to do so many things together."

"This won't ruin the summer," Tarah insisted. "Me and Coop have all kinds of things planned. We gonna be at the beach all the time, havin' cookouts, and dancin'. It'll be lotsa of fun."

"Tarah," Darcy wailed, "don't you understand? I can't just forget about Hakeem!"

"Girl, I ain't tellin' you to forget about him. You can write him letters, and you can call him, too," Tarah said. "But, don't stop your life, girl. You ain't even a junior. You can't act like a widow. Besides, if you don't stop all that crying soon, your eyeballs are gonna fall out of your head."

Darcy smiled. "Thanks, Tarah," she said, wrapping her arms around her friend. Just then, the bell sounded, signaling the end of the lunch period. Darcy and Tarah quickly headed into the hallway to get to their next class.

"It'll be okay, girl. You'll see," Tarah said, as she turned down a separate corridor.

Darcy was grateful for her friend's support, but as she watched Tarah disappear in a crowd of students, she knew there would be more tears ahead.

After school, Darcy went straight to Liselle's apartment. It was her first day babysitting Kelena.

"Hey, Darcy," Liselle said, opening the apartment door. "Come on in." As Darcy entered, Liselle grabbed a backpack from a nearby table. "Kelena is asleep in her crib. I left two bottles of milk in the fridge, some snacks on the kitchen counter, and there's a box of toys right next to the crib," Liselle explained.

"We'll be fine," Darcy replied. "You just concentrate on school, and don't worry about me and Kelena."

"I'm kinda nervous about goin' back," Liselle admitted. "I been out for so long, everything might sound like a different language to me."

"Liselle, you're gonna do great," Darcy said enthusiastically. "You'll be at the head of your class in no time."

"Girl, I hope so. This is my chance to make a better life for me and my baby. I owe it to her, to both of us," Liselle said, glancing toward Kelena's crib.

"You're a good mom," Darcy said sincerely. "And, I'm sure Kelena's gonna be real proud of you one day."

"Thanks, Darcy." Liselle smiled and took a deep breath. "Well, I want to get there a little early on my first day. Maybe that'll calm these nerves down." She waved goodbye and headed out the door.

Darcy then went to check on Kelena. The baby was sleeping soundly, so Darcy tiptoed back into the small living room, grabbed her history textbook from her backpack, and sat on the couch. After several minutes of silence, she heard someone inserting a key into the door lock.

It must be Liselle, Darcy thought. *She probably forgot a book or something.* Quickly, Darcy went to open the door. As she turned the knob, the door pushed open from the other side, and Brian Mason stood before her.

"Hi, Brian," Darcy said, unsure of what else to say. Liselle had not mentioned he would be coming.

"What's up, Darcy?" he said with a smile. "I almost forgot you'd be here today."

Quickly, she backed away from the door so he could come into the apartment. "It's my first day on the job," Darcy explained. "I just got here a little while ago." She could smell Brian's cologne, strong, but pleasant. He was wearing baggy black jeans, boots, and a snug black T-shirt, which emphasized his broad shoulders. *He is really handsome,* Darcy thought. "Aren't you working today?" she asked.

"Yeah," he answered, walking into the apartment with his hands behind his back. "I have to get to work, but I wanted to give you something for your first day here." He pulled his arm from behind his back and gave Darcy a single red rose. "For you."

For an instant, Darcy was speechless. She could not believe Brian was giving something so nice to her.

"Oh my goodness!" she exclaimed. "A rose! But, why?"

"Because you're one beautiful girl," Brian said. "And because it's your first day sittin' with the baby. Consider it a thank you from me, Kelena, and my sister."

Darcy took the rose. "Thank you, Brian. It's beautiful." The delicate petals felt like red velvet in Darcy's fingers.

"Well, I gotta go to work, Darcy. I just wanted to leave you with something special today," he said, turning toward the door. "I'll see you again soon." Then he walked out.

In the quiet of the empty living room, Darcy examined the rose. No one, not Hakeem or anyone else, had ever given her a flower. Twirling the stem in her fingers, Darcy felt a thorn prick her thumb.

"Ouch," she cried, as a tiny bead of blood appeared where the thorn had stabbed her.

Sucking the salty blood from her thumb, Darcy wondered about Brian. Had he given her the flower just to be nice, or did the rose mean something more?

Chapter 4

Looking at the red rose in her hand, Darcy wondered what Hakeem would say if she told him about Brian's present. *Of course, the rose doesn't mean anything. It's just a friendly gift,* Darcy assured herself. *But would Hakeem feel the same way?*

A tinge of guilt crept into Darcy's mind. She figured Hakeem might be jealous if he knew about the flower, and she did not want to give him anything more to worry about. But the idea of hiding it from him seemed dishonest. What bothered her more was how much she enjoyed that Brian had given it to her. Darcy knew she could not tell Hakeem that.

Liselle returned from school several hours later. Darcy was playing with

Kelena when she heard the door open.

"Girl, if the first day was this hard, I don't know how I'm gonna make it through the rest of the semester," Liselle said wearily. Her eyes focused on the rose on the table.

"It's from Brian," Darcy explained, "He said it was a thank you from all of you." Liselle's face twisted into an expression that Darcy could not read. Uncomfortable with the awkward silence, Darcy quickly changed the subject. "Kelena's been an angel," Darcy said.

"Thanks a million, Darcy," Liselle replied, her face becoming more relaxed. "I just don't know what I'd do without you."

"Don't mention it," Darcy said. "So, I'll see you the day after tomorrow."

Walking out of the apartment, Darcy grabbed the rose and held it close to her chest. She wondered why Liselle acted so strangely when she noticed the flower.

At home, Darcy put the rose in a tall vase and placed it on her bedroom windowsill. Then she joined Dad and Jamee in the kitchen, where Dad was preparing dinner and Jamee was helping him. They were laughing together when Darcy entered. "You call that chopped green pepper?" Dad teased. "It looks more like mashed pepper."

"Yeah, well, you left so many lumps in the mashed potatoes, we should call them lumped potatoes," Jamee said, laughing. For a second, Darcy felt as if she had stepped back in time. Jamee and Dad's laughter reminded Darcy of the days before Dad left. Back then, family meals were sacred, and each Sunday Dad cooked something special he had learned from his years working in restaurants. Vivid memories of the past swirled in the air with the scent of Dad's pork chops in red cajun sauce.

"Hey, baby." Dad smiled at Darcy. "I hope you brought an appetite with you. We got enough food here for an army, and Mom's workin' late tonight again."

Dad's work schedule at the store gave him two days off in mid-week. Since the week Jamee ran away months ago, he had made an effort to spend those days making meals for the family. It was as if he tried to make up for years of lost family dinners by cooking each week.

"Well, I'm starvin' for some mashed peppers and lumpy potatoes," Darcy joked as she sat down at the kitchen table. She looked around and noticed that her grandmother was missing. "Where's Grandma?" she asked.

"She's restin' in her room," Dad said. "Grandma isn't feelin' well today."

"She's been in bed since I came home from school," Jamee added, exchanging a concerned glance with her father.

A wave of sadness washed over Darcy. Recently, she noticed that her grandmother's health seemed to be declining. Darcy clung to the hope that Grandma would bounce back to her former self, but with each passing day, it seemed less and less likely.

Dad and Jamee joined Darcy at the table. Before eating, Dad blessed the food and announced that Mom was considering taking a part-time position at the hospital.

"Did she really say she would?" Darcy asked, surprised.

"Well, she's thinking about it," Dad said. "She's thinking hard on it."

"Isn't that great, Darce?" Jamee said. "Then Mom will get to be home more, and we could eat together, just like we used to."

Darcy nodded. Her mind raced with memories of how her mother had suffered after Dad left. Darcy wondered if it would be the same for her if Hakeem moved away.

"Darcy, you okay?" Dad asked. "You seem like you're someplace else."

"No, no." Darcy smiled weakly. "I'm fine. Dinner looks great," she added, hoping to change the subject. She saw Dad eyeing her carefully, but he said nothing.

After the dishes were done, Darcy mustered up the courage to dial Hakeem's number. She felt her heart pound as she pressed each of the digits. She did not know what she was going to say, but she had to speak to him. The phone rang twice before Hakeem's mother answered. "Hello?" she said, her voice tense.

"Hi," Darcy said. "May I speak to Hakeem, please?"

"Just a minute," Hakeem's mother sighed as if she were relieved and annoyed at the same time.

Darcy's hands trembled as she waited for him to pick up the phone. After several agonizing seconds, Hakeem's voice came through the other end.

"Hello?"

"Hakeem," Darcy began in a shaky voice, "I'm sorry to bother you, but—"

"Darcy, I can't talk right now," Hakeem said. "I'm sorry, but we're expecting a call from my uncle."

"Is there any time we *can* talk?" Darcy asked, hating how desperate her voice sounded.

Hakeem hesitated and then replied, "I'll call you tomorrow night, okay? I promise."

"Okay," Darcy replied.

"Thanks for understanding. Gotta go," Hakeem said and hung up the phone.

Darcy stared at the phone for a while before hanging it up, her eyes wet with tears.

On Saturday morning, Darcy woke up feeling depressed. Unable to reach Tarah over the phone, she decided to stay home the entire day. Closing her bedroom door, she started to unpack the boxes that remained in her room from the previous week's move.

For several hours, she put up posters, organized her closet and arranged her tiny wooden desk. She even placed her one picture of Hakeem next to her bed the way it had been in her old room.

In one old box, she also discovered a tattered photograph of her grandmother taken many years ago. The sight of Grandma so young and strong only added to Darcy's sorrow.

At noon, the phone rang, and Darcy answered it.

"Hey girl, can you do me a favor?" a woman's voice asked. Immediately Darcy knew it was Liselle. Before Darcy had a chance to reply, Liselle explained that she needed extra time to study at the local library. Reluctantly, Darcy agreed to watch the baby.

"Thanks for comin' by on such short notice," Liselle said when Darcy arrived. A full backpack hung heavily from Liselle's shoulder. "By the way, Brian's working until 6:00 so you don't have to worry about him bugging you," Liselle added and paused thoughtfully. "You do have a boyfriend, right?"

"Yeah," Darcy replied, surprised by the question.

"Good," Liselle sighed, as if what Darcy said had somehow calmed her. "So, y'all been going together for a long time?"

"Six months," Darcy said, wondering why Liselle was so curious.

"You go, girl!" Liselle exclaimed. "I'm happy you got someone special. You deserve it. Just be careful and make sure you protect yourself. You don't wanna end up like I did, seventeen and pregnant."

"We never . . . um . . . I mean, we don't have anything to worry about," Darcy stammered, a bit surprised by Liselle's frankness. "His family might be moving away in the next week or two. I'm not sure what's going to happen with us this summer."

"Really?" Liselle said. For an instant, Darcy thought Liselle's face tensed up, but just as quickly, the look on her face vanished. "Well, don't worry. If he's the right one, you'll see him again." Liselle glanced at the clock on the wall as she spoke. "Well, I gotta get to the library. Bye, Darcy." Liselle grabbed her keys and headed out the door.

Darcy sat down in the small living room. She could not figure out why Liselle suddenly seemed so interested in her personal life. Darcy wanted to believe that Liselle was just being friendly. But her instinct told her that something else was going on. But what?

And what about Liselle's comment about Hakeem? Darcy wondered. *'If he's the right one, you'll see him again.'* The words were still running through Darcy's mind as she walked back to her house later that afternoon.

When Darcy got home, she went to Grandma's room, where Jamee was pulling the covers up for Grandma. "Hi, Darce," Jamee said. "Can you stay here with Grandma for a while? Dad and I want to do some shopping at the supermarket."

"Sure, go ahead. I'm not going anywhere," Darcy answered glumly. After they left, she sat with Grandma, gazing out of the bedroom window as heavy gray clouds gathered overhead.

Darcy hoped Hakeem would call. Each time the phone rang, Darcy rushed to answer it, thinking it was him. But instead, the calls were from Jamee's friends. Before long, Darcy heard Dad and Jamee return from the store. She went into the kitchen and found them both carrying large bags stuffed with groceries.

"Dad bought all this healthy stuff, Darce," Jamee laughed. "Like he's training for the Olympics or somethin'." They began sorting the food, putting canned vegetables in the cupboards, and the meats, fresh vegetables, and fruits into the refrigerator.

"Hey," Dad said, "I'm tryin' to get down to fightin' trim, like I was in the army. I've lost almost fifteen pounds since I been back. I hope I can keep it off." Darcy noticed Dad was watching her closely. "You all right, Darcy?" he asked.

"I'm fine," she replied, glancing at her father in his T-shirt and blue jeans. She could see that he had lost weight. He looked ten years younger than he did when he first came back. Looking at him, Darcy remembered what Liselle had said about seeing Hakeem again. *If Dad could come back,* Darcy hoped, *maybe Hakeem might too.*

"You sure everything's okay?" he asked.

"Everything's fine, Dad. I just have lots of studying to do for exams," she said and then retreated into her room. As she closed her bedroom door, she noticed the rose Brian had given her. It was now the size of a fist, its blood-red petals fully opened and blooming. Staring at the flower, Darcy waited for Hakeem's call. At 8:00 the phone rang, and she rushed to the kitchen to answer it.

"Hello?" she asked, nervous to speak to Hakeem.

"Darcy, it's Brian. Is it too late to call?"

"No, it's fine," she said, surprised to hear Brian's voice.

"I hope you don't mind me callin' you," he said. "I got your phone number from my sister."

"No, I don't mind," Darcy said. "So what's up?"

"I wanted to know what you're doing tomorrow. I was thinking maybe we could get together sometime, you know, so we can talk without me having to rush off."

Darcy's heart skipped a beat. "That sounds nice, Brian, but I've gotta study for final exams tomorrow," Darcy replied. "Maybe we could do something when the school year ends and things settle down."

"Sounds cool," Brian said calmly. "Well, you know where to find me. I'll see you next time you babysit."

Darcy said goodbye and hung up. Returning to her bedroom, she imagined what it would be like to spend the afternoon with Brian. As much as she did not want to admit it, the idea of seeing him interested her. Feeling a pang of guilt, she forced the thought into the back of her mind and waited for Hakeem to call. But as the evening grew later and later, the phone did not ring.

But he promised he would call, Darcy thought as she struggled to stay awake late into the evening. *He promised me.*

Chapter 5

On Sunday, Darcy awoke to a gray and dreary morning. Steady rain pelted her window, and a thick mist hung like a heavy wet blanket over her street.

Sitting up in bed, Darcy looked at the picture of Hakeem she had unpacked the day before. The photo was taken one early spring afternoon when he came along with her as she wheeled Grandma to a nearby park. In the photo, Hakeem was smiling widely. Darcy recalled that earlier that day, he had put his arm around her back as they walked. Though only a few months old, the photo seemed as if it was from a time long gone. Just seeing it twisted Darcy's chest into a painful knot of anger, sadness, and frustration.

How could this happen? Darcy thought. She and Hakeem had been through so much together, and they had always helped each other. Now it seemed Hakeem was letting go of everything. Other couples break up, Darcy thought. But that was not supposed to happen to her and Hakeem. They were different.

Darcy struggled through her studies for several hours and then went to her grandmother's room. Grandma was sitting in her wheelchair watching a small bird on her windowsill.

"Hi, Grandma."

"Hi, Angelcake," Grandma said cheerfully, her eyes glimmering brightly, contrasting with the dull weather outside. Months had passed since Darcy had seen her grandmother so alert. "Is something wrong?" Grandma asked, her wrinkled forehead shriveling into an expression of worry.

"I just have a lot of studying to do, that's all," Darcy said.

"Angelcake, you're gonna pass all those exams with flying colors. Ain't a cloud in the sky that can steal your sunshine," Grandma said.

"Thanks, Grandma." For an instant, Darcy considered telling her grandmother about Hakeem. Just a few years ago, Darcy would have explained everything to her. As a child, Darcy would lie on Grandma's lap and talk about all her troubles. But all that ended with Grandma's stroke. Since then, her grandmother's health changed like the weather, and somebody always had to be home to care for her.

"You're a wonderful granddaughter, Angelcake. You're gonna be okay," Grandma said.

"Thank you, Grandma," Darcy said and hugged her. As she walked out, Darcy said a silent prayer that there would be more days she and Grandma could spend together.

As she finished up her studying that night, Darcy wondered what she would say to Hakeem when she saw him. For the first time she could remember, Darcy was angry at him. She knew the next time she saw him that they would have to talk. He owed her that much, she thought.

Darcy looked for Hakeem Monday morning in the Bluford parking lot but did not see him. At lunchtime, she sat with Tarah and told her how upset she was that Hakeem had not called.

"Just remember what I said," Tarah explained. "He's having a difficult time right now, so you gotta cut him some slack."

"I'm trying, Tarah, but he won't even tell me what's happening. What am I supposed to do?"

"Like I said, don't stop livin' your life. The only reason Hakeem's actin' this way is 'cause he's got his hands full with his family. Just let him take care of what he's got to do, and he'll come around. You can't just sit around mopin' 'cause that don't get you nowhere."

Darcy nodded. She knew Tarah was right, and she felt guilty for being so angry. But she was also frustrated that Hakeem did not even talk to her.

"All this studyin' is cloggin' up my brain," Tarah said, leafing through a purple notebook. "Girl, I'm gettin' everything all mixed up. Math is lookin' like history, and history is lookin' like biology. I just don't know how I'm gonna get through this week."

"Yeah, neither do I," Darcy mumbled, though to her, exams seemed easy compared with everything else.

"By the way, Darce," Tarah started, pausing as though she was choosing her words carefully, "you might not want to talk about this right now, but me and

Coop were thinkin' about throwin' Hakeem a little going-away party on Saturday. We were talkin' about goin' to his favorite pizza place, Niko's. Just the four of us, like old times."

"Oh," Darcy said, feeling her heart rise into her throat. The words "going-away" seemed to hang in the air. "That sounds really nice. Um, let me see what I've got planned for that day."

"What you've got planned for that day?" Tarah asked, raising her voice. "Your boyfriend's going-away party? Of course you'll be there. Why wouldn't you?"

"I'll try to be there, Tarah," Darcy explained. "But, I might have something else to do that day, that's all. Liselle might need me to sit with the baby, or Mom might need me to look after Grandma. I'll let you know in advance, though."

"Well, please do, Miss Darcy," Tarah said sarcastically. "Let me know when you can find a minute for us in your very busy schedule. I mean, we're only your best friends."

"I'm sorry, Tarah," Darcy said, putting her hand over Tarah's. "It's just that I can't think about Hakeem going away. I'm just not ready to deal with it, you know. I keep hoping that something will change and he'll be able to stay."

"Oh, girl," Tarah said warmly. "It doesn't have to be over. Give this thing time, Darcy, and stop expectin' the end of the world. Right now, we gotta deal with what's real. And what's real is that Hakeem is movin' to Detroit. That don't mean forever. But it does mean that we don't have much time to say goodbye. Now what's the best thing we can do with so little time? The way I see it, we should have fun like we used to do. That's why you should be with us."

"I know you're right, but I'm not sure—"

"Darcy, I'll be really disappointed if you don't show up. We're your friends," Tarah said.

"I know, Tarah, but I wouldn't expect you to be happy if Cooper moved away," Darcy replied sharply, heading to her next class.

When Darcy got home, she heard Grandma calling, "Angelcake!"

"I'm coming," Darcy answered, heading towards the bedroom.

"I need to go to the bathroom,"

Grandma said, reaching for her walker. Darcy grabbed it and helped her grandmother to her feet. Grandma was unusually wobbly. Darcy steadied her and carefully helped her get to the bathroom and then back to bed. Grandma walked slowly, mumbling at one point, "I can't go no further. I gotta sit down and rest."

"It's okay," Darcy assured her. "Just a few more steps. We're almost there."

Once she was back in bed, Grandma huffed wearily as Darcy helped to cover her. "That's better. Now you just rest." Darcy watched as Grandma slowly closed her eyes and drifted off to sleep. She had never seen her grandmother look more frail and helpless.

Darcy closed her eyes briefly, and distant memories flooded her mind. In flashes, she could see Grandma playing with her as a small child, helping with homework, and later supporting Mom when Dad ran out on the family. In all her childhood memories, Darcy never imagined her grandmother would become so weak and vulnerable.

A deep sadness swept over Darcy as the memories streamed through her mind. She could almost feel time passing, and yet she was powerless to stop it.

While the year had brought her a new home and the return of her father, it also threatened two people Darcy loved— Grandma and Hakeem.

During the next few days, Bluford's corridors seemed charged with tension. Some students wandered the halls looking frazzled from last-minute cramming for their final exams. Others seemed energized by the warm weather and the knowledge that summer vacation was only days away.

Although Darcy hated studying for finals, she was glad to have something to distract her from her worries.

"Well, we've gotten through three days already," Darcy said when she saw Tarah and Cooper in the cafeteria. "Just today and tomorrow to go."

"Girl, I don't know," Tarah said, in between sips of a soda. "This stuff ain't easy. I don't know how much more I can take. The weekend can't get here fast enough."

Just then Darcy spotted Hakeem approaching the lunch table. She nearly spilled her drink when she saw him. They had not seen each other in days, and since their last phone conversation, she had given up trying to call. Instead, she waited for him to talk to her.

"Hey, look who it is," Cooper said as Hakeem pulled up a chair at the table. The two boys slapped hands as Hakeem sat down wearily. Darcy noticed immediately that Hakeem was avoiding eye contact with her. "How are your exams goin'?" Cooper asked.

"Okay, I think. It's kinda hard to study with everything that's been goin' on."

"I heard that," Cooper said. "But I always got trouble with exams. The only one who don't is Einstein over here," Cooper said, pointing to Darcy.

"It's true," Tarah added. "Nobody studies as much as you do. But no one does better neither."

Darcy forced a smile. She was not in the mood to be the center of attention. All she wanted was to talk to Hakeem, alone.

For a second the table was unnaturally quiet. Darcy could sense that Tarah and Cooper knew she was upset and were trying to figure out what to talk about.

"So, we all gettin' together Saturday night?" Cooper asked, looking at Darcy.

"Uh," Darcy said, unsure what to say. "Yeah, sure."

"It's gonna be fun, y'all," Tarah said, seeming as if Darcy's response relaxed her.

"Just like old times," Cooper said, dumping a thick red glob of ketchup on Tarah's plate of french fries.

Darcy glanced at Hakeem. But as soon as she caught his eye, she turned away. She could not hide how sad she felt and did not want to start crying in the middle of the crowded cafeteria.

"Can we talk after school?" Hakeem asked. "Just the two of us?"

"Sure." Darcy nodded, looking down at the table.

"I'll meet you in the parking lot after last period," Hakeem said.

For the rest of the day, time seemed to race. Sitting in her last class, Darcy could almost feel each precious second stream by and vanish. Even the boring moments in class would soon be gone. One day, Darcy suspected, she would want even them back.

Struggling to sit still, Darcy knew she would endure a year of boring days at Bluford if only Hakeem would stay right where he was. Her thoughts were shattered at the sound of the final bell. Everyone bolted from their desks, and Darcy headed for the parking lot.

Hakeem was there, leaning against his silver motorbike. "Hey, Darce," he said when she reached him. "Thanks for meeting me," he continued, fidgeting with his fingers and rubbing his hands on his face.

"How have you been?" Darcy asked, unsure how to begin talking to him after so much time had passed.

"Darcy," Hakeem replied, pausing to take a deep breath. "We need to talk."

Darcy felt a knot in her stomach. "What is it?"

"It's about us," Hakeem mumbled somberly, as if he could barely force the words out. "I've been thinkin' about what's gonna happen when I move to Detroit, and I know we haven't really talked about it that much but—"

"Hakeem, what are you trying to say?"

"With all that's been goin' on lately, I just feel like we should cool things down. I mean I don't think I can do this anymore, not with everything else, you know?"

For a second, Darcy was speechless. She felt as if she could not possibly have heard him correctly, that there must have been a mistake. There was just no way Hakeem could give up on her, she thought. Not after all this time. Not after what Tarah said. No way.

"What are you saying?" Darcy blurted out, her voice rising as she spoke. "Why can't we call and write? Maybe we'll be able to visit on breaks from school. Maybe we'll even—"

"Darcy, I'm not saying we won't stay in touch," Hakeem explained. "But right now, with Dad sick and Mom stressed out, I can't handle this, you know. It's like everyone is pulling me in different directions, and there just ain't enough of me to go around," he added taking a deep breath. "And it's not gonna get any easier when I move. I think we need to cool things down, that's all."

"What does that *mean*? Are you breaking up with me?"

Hakeem turned away from her. "Darcy, it's not 'cause I want to, but . . . y-yeah . . . I-I am," he stammered.

Darcy shook her head in disbelief. Hurt and anger swirled together in her mind, making her heart pound and her body tremble. "I can't believe you're doing this after all we've been through," Darcy yelled. "How can you *do* this?"

Hakeem lowered his head, shrugged his shoulders, and sighed. "I'm sorry, Darcy," he said finally. "There's way too much goin' on with my dad and with moving and that whole thing. I hope you can understand this, Darcy—"

"Well, I don't," Darcy said. "I've been doing nothing but trying to understand you for weeks now. When you didn't return my phone calls, I tried to understand. When you avoided me in school, I tried to understand. I'm not stupid, and I know things are difficult for you, but I don't understand why you've been treating me this way. And this? After all we've been through, I don't understood this at all!"

"Darcy, calm down," Hakeem pleaded. "It doesn't have to end like this."

"Yes it does! That's what you said, right?!" Darcy snapped. "Did you think you could just dump me and I wouldn't be upset?" She paused briefly, fighting the sorrow building in her chest. "I never would have walked out on *you*, Hakeem. And you know what else? I never would have guessed that you'd do this to me."

Tears of anger and hurt stung Darcy's eyes as she turned and stormed away.

"Darcy, I'm sorry," Hakeem said again as she left, but she did not turn to face him. Instead, she ran, first out of the Bluford High parking lot, then down the neighboring street, and through groups of students who parted to let her pass. The more Darcy ran, the more she cried. Hot, salty tears streamed from her eyes and snaked across her cheeks into her hair. Darcy finally stopped at a small park, leaned against a tree, and buried her face in her hands.

It's over, she thought. Hakeem and she were no longer together. Everything she feared was true. Wiping her eyes, Darcy heard a vehicle slowly approaching the curb near her. She was certain Hakeem was coming to talk to her. Quickly, she dried her eyes to hide that she had been crying.

"You okay, Darcy?" asked a voice much deeper than Hakeem's. "I saw you sprintin' down the street."

Darcy turned to see Brian sitting in his Toyota. "I'm fine," she answered awkwardly, embarrassed that he was seeing her in such a state.

Brian stepped out of his car and walked over to her. Before she knew it, he had put his arm around her shoulder. "I'll take you home," he said gently.

"I'm all right. I just had a fight with my boyfriend. I mean my ex-boyfriend," Darcy said bitterly, shrugging her shoulders.

"Do you want to tell me about it?"

Darcy looked up at Brian. His dark and piercing eyes glimmered in the afternoon sun. For a second, Darcy was tempted to tell him everything that happened, about how Hakeem had just walked out of her life, about how her hopes for the summer were gone. But she did not feel right telling Brian, not now. "Maybe some other time," she mumbled.

"Anybody who would let go of you has got to be stupid," Brian said. "You sure you don't want a ride home?" Darcy glanced at Brian, and he gestured toward his car and grinned. "Come on," he urged. "It's not gonna bite you."

Darcy smiled and got into the car. Within minutes the Toyota was in front of Darcy's house.

"Thanks for bringing me home," Darcy said. "That was really nice of you."

"No big thing," Brian replied, and

then added, "If you ever need to talk, I'm here. I mean that. Anytime."

Darcy stepped out of the car slowly. "Thanks again, Brian," she said. Somehow her fight with Hakeem no longer felt as raw. As she opened the front door to her house, she looked back at Brian. He waved once, and drove off.

Watching his car disappear down the street, Darcy felt a heavy wave of sadness sweep across her heart, sadness for Hakeem and the end of their relationship. But even as the sorrow gathered in her chest, she felt something else, something she did not want to admit to anyone, not even herself.

Darcy knew something inside had changed, making the loss of Hakeem seem less sharp and more bearable. Closing the door behind her, Darcy knew the change had to do with Brian.

Chapter 6

The last day of school had finally come. Fog blazed brightly in the morning sun as Darcy reluctantly made her way toward Bluford. Nearing the high school, she heard several students talking about how glad they were that exams were over and that summer vacation was about to begin. Darcy wished she felt as they did, but to her, the summer was coming too quickly. Hakeem would be gone in days. Even though he had broken up with her, Darcy still hated that he was leaving, and that things had turned out so horribly between them.

When she reached her locker, Darcy saw Brisana Meeks heading in her direction. Darcy rolled her eyes and hoped she would pass by, but Brisana came right to her.

"Hi, Darcy," Brisana said, with a

tight-lipped smirk. "Aren't you glad the school year's over? I couldn't take another day in this place."

"Yeah, I know what you mean," Darcy replied cautiously. She did not feel like talking to Brisana about anything, especially not Hakeem.

"Well, I just wanted to make sure everything's okay with you. I mean, I saw you with Brian again the other day, and you looked really upset," she said.

"*So?*" Darcy challenged. "What's it to you?"

"Why are you getting so mad? I just wanted to make sure you're okay, you know, with Hakeem and Brian and everything."

"I'm fine, Brisana!" Darcy snapped. "When did you become so interested in my personal life?"

"What do you mean?" Brisana asked. "Can't I try and make conversation with you?"

"Well, it's just that you don't seem to want that," Darcy said, closing her locker door.

Brisana stepped back and glared at Darcy. "How would you know what I want?" she yelled. "Maybe I act that way because you never give me a chance.

You're always with Tarah, and I never get a word in edgewise when I try to talk to you."

Darcy did not know what to say. She was not sure whether Brisana was serious. "I'm sorry, Brisana. There's a lot going on right now, you know? It's hard to talk about everything," Darcy explained.

"I know," Brisana said, moving closer to Darcy. "But there's something I need to tell you, something important. I think you should be very careful with Brian Mason," Brisana said slowly. "I know things about him, things that other people might not know. I tried to tell you before, but you—"

"I don't want to hear it!" Darcy snapped. Now she knew what Brisana was after—Brian. Like so many times before, Brisana was trying to stir up trouble. But it wouldn't work, Darcy thought. "Bye," she said abruptly.

"Darcy, just listen for one minute—"

"That's it, Brisana. I can't talk right now, okay? I've gotta go," Darcy snapped, turning away. As she headed down the hallway, Darcy glanced back to see Brisana still standing by her locker. Her mouth hung open, as if she had just been slapped.

At the end of the day, Darcy and Tarah arrived at their lockers at the same time. "Hey, girl," said Tarah. "You're just the one I want to see. How 'bout goin' to the mall?"

"Thanks anyway, Tarah, but I don't feel up to it. I'm just not in the mood to be around a bunch of happy people right now."

"Then why don't you at least ask Hakeem for a ride home? You two are still friends, right?" Tarah asked.

"I don't have anything more to say to him, Tarah," Darcy replied bitterly. "Not after the way he broke up with me. Besides, he doesn't have anything to say to me either. He already told me everything I need to know."

"I know you're upset, but don't let that ruin your friendship. You gotta come to the party tomorrow, and set things straight with him," Tarah said.

"I'll let you know tomorrow," Darcy replied before walking to the exit. Descending the front stairs of the high school, Darcy remembered countless times she had walked the same steps with Hakeem. Despite her anger, she could not imagine Bluford without him.

Outside, the sun blazed, warming the streets and sidewalk. Darcy walked away from the school quickly, trying to ignore the nice weather, which only seemed to mock her feelings. As she approached her house, a familiar voice jarred her out of her thoughts.

"What's up, Darcy?"

She turned to see Brian sitting in his red Toyota next to the curb. "Hi, Brian," she said. "What are you doing here?"

"My boss changed my schedule and gave me the rest of the afternoon off. I thought maybe I'd catch you here and we could go to the beach or something."

Darcy hesitated. She did not want to be rude to Brian, but it seemed strange to go out with him, especially to the beach. The only boy who had ever taken her there was Hakeem.

"Thanks, Brian, but—"

"Come on, Darcy," he insisted. "I promise I'll have you back early. Besides, it's your last day of school, so you should do something special."

Darcy smiled, unsure of what to say. She did not feel like going home and sitting in the living room while the rest of the world was outside. "How is it that you always seem to be around whenever I'm walking home?"

"Good timing, I guess," he replied with a grin. "So do you wanna join me?"

He was wearing his navy-blue security uniform. As Darcy watched, he unbuttoned his dark-blue shirt to reveal a tight gray T-shirt underneath.

"Okay," Darcy agreed. "As long as I'm back by 5:00."

"Hop in," Brian said.

Darcy climbed into the Toyota and immediately noticed the heavy scent of Brian's cologne. His T-shirt clung tightly to his muscular shoulders, and when he steered the car, his thick forearms rippled with muscle. Darcy did not want him to notice her staring at him. "Thanks for picking me up the other day," she said, shifting her eyes straight ahead. "You really helped me out just by being there."

"It was nothing, Darcy," Brian said. "I was just worried about you, you know, with the fight with your boyfriend. I mean *ex-boyfriend*," he added, turning toward her briefly.

"Yeah, I'm sorry I was so upset. I still can't believe he broke up with me."

"Well that's *his* loss, Darcy."

The car traveled the familiar highway to the ocean. The beach was one of the first places she had ever gone with Hakeem. It felt unnatural to be heading there with anyone else, especially another guy. Yet in a way, she was excited to be there.

When they arrived at the shore, Darcy was glad to see that Brian drove to a different part of the beach than she had gone to with Hakeem. "Right here," he said. "This is my favorite spot."

The beach was rocky and secluded. It was as if they were on some exotic land, looking at an ocean she had never seen before. Scanning the beach, Darcy noticed they were almost completely alone.

"Isn't it nice here?" Brian said.

"It's beautiful," Darcy answered, nodding.

Brian stepped close to Darcy so that his chest was just behind her shoulder. She could almost feel his eyes gazing down at her. "Then it matches you," he said.

Darcy turned to look at Brian. Her heart started to pound, and she suddenly felt clumsy and awkward. She did not know what to say. Part of her felt guilty just for being at the beach with him. But another part of her was thrilled. For an instant, her mouth become as dry as beach sand, and she wondered whether she would even be able to speak. But she could not endure the tense silence.

"You wanna go for a walk?" she asked finally, hoping Brian could not see how nervous she was.

"Sure," he said, taking a deep breath and smiling.

As they strolled towards the water, Brian briefly placed his hand on Darcy's back to steady her on a slippery rock. His touch was warm and unexpected, and she felt the pressure of each of his fingers against the muscles in her back.

Though it lasted just a second, Darcy still felt Brian's touch hours later. Though she would not admit it, as she closed her eyes that night, Darcy hoped she would see him again soon.

The next morning, Darcy was awakened by Jamee's voice.

"Darcy, get up. Tarah's on the phone."

"Tell her I'll call her back later," Darcy said with a yawn. But throughout the day, Darcy avoided returning Tarah's call. She even refused to answer the phone whenever it rang, fearing it would be Tarah.

Darcy knew Tarah was calling about Hakeem's going-away party that evening. As much as she cared about Hakeem, Darcy did not want to spend several hours pretending to be happy when all she felt was sadness. And then there was Brian. The time at the beach with him confused her. She had never mentioned him to Tarah or Hakeem, and as she thought about her old friends, a gnawing pang of guilt sunk deep in her chest.

At 4:00, the phone rang again, and Darcy ignored it until Jamee yelled out, "Darcy, can you get that? I'm sitting with Grandma."

Reluctantly, Darcy picked it up. "Hello?" she grunted.

"Girl, where you been at?" Tarah asked. "I called you early this morning, and your sister said you'd call me back. I been waitin' to hear from you for hours."

"Yeah, she said you called. Sorry, Tarah," Darcy responded, taking a deep breath. "I . . . wanted to . . . tell you that—"

"Darcy," Tarah interrupted. "What's goin' on? Whatcha tryin' to tell me? Spit it out, girl. We got a party to go to."

"Tarah, I can't go to the party," Darcy said finally.

"You what?"

"I just can't do it, Tarah. Hakeem already said goodbye to me when he decided we needed to break up. I haven't seen or spoken to him since, and I don't think I can. Not at a party. There's no way I can sit with you all tonight and pretend to be happy. Do you understand?" As Darcy spoke, she wanted to tell Tarah more, to mention Brian and the guilt she felt for having such a good time with him. But she could not form the words.

For a minute, Tarah was silent, and Darcy listened to the electronic hum of the quiet phone line. With each passing second, the silence became more unbearable, and Darcy felt a nervous knot in her stomach as she waited for her friend's reply.

"Okay, Darcy," Tarah said finally, taking a deep breath. "If you don't want to come, that's fine. The three of us will go without you."

"I hope you understand, Tarah," Darcy explained. "I don't want you to be mad at me."

"Darcy, I ain't mad at you," Tarah

replied. "This is not between me and you. This is between you and the person you might never see again. Whatever went wrong, you don't have much longer to make it right. That's all I have to say. Talk to you later, girl."

Tarah hung up, and Darcy stood motionless holding the buzzing phone in her hand. Deep inside, she knew Tarah was right, but she could not bring herself to be with Hakeem, especially not with other people around. But as Darcy thought about Tarah's words, she knew she had to see Hakeem one more time, alone. This time she would say goodbye forever.

On Monday morning, Darcy got dressed quickly. She knew Hakeem's family was leaving early for Detroit, and she wanted to see him before he left. While the morning fog still hung thick over the neighborhood, Darcy walked the eight blocks to his house.

Turning onto Hakeem's street, she saw a large yellow moving truck in front of his house. A nervous tremor raced up her spine as she made her way down the familiar block. She wondered how Hakeem would react when he saw her.

Near the house, Darcy spotted Hakeem's father trying to carry a package into the truck. He was much thinner than the last time Darcy saw him, and the effort to move the box seemed to exhaust him.

Walking up to the driveway, Darcy was surprised at how much older Hakeem's father appeared. She was about to help him when Hakeem suddenly emerged from the house.

"Here, Dad, let me carry that," he said. "Go inside and sit down." Hakeem grabbed the box easily and led his father back into the house.

Darcy felt a rush of guilt. She had not fully realized how sick Hakeem's father was. One look at his withered body told her what a heavy burden Hakeem and his family were under. She wished she had never gotten so upset at him.

The front door of the house opened again, and Hakeem stepped into the driveway still carrying the box he had taken from his father. He nearly dropped it when he saw her.

"Darcy?"

For a second, Darcy was motionless, but then she walked over to him. "Hi," she said awkwardly, unsure of where to begin. "So I guess this is the big day."

"Yeah," Hakeem replied with a weary nod, putting the box down. "Look, Darcy, about the other day. I might not have said things the right way. I'm really sorry—"

"It's okay," Darcy interjected. "You don't need to apologize, and I didn't come here to get into all that. I came here to say goodbye."

"Darcy," Hakeem said, shaking his head. "I'm gonna miss you, girl."

"Me too, Hakeem," Darcy said, staring into his dark eyes.

"Hakeem! Can you move this box?" Hakeem's mother shouted from inside the house.

"I guess this is it," Hakeem said, ignoring his mother.

Darcy nodded, but said nothing. She could feel tears gathering in her eyes. She stepped toward him, and in one swift motion, he opened his arms and wrapped them around her. Enfolded in his embrace, Darcy remembered her months with Hakeem and all the wonderful times she had with him. She wished the moment would never end, but the sound of Hakeem's mother yelling told her it had to.

"Hakeem! I need you to move this box," his mother called out again, an impatient edge to her voice.

"Will we see each other again?" Darcy asked in a whisper.

"I don't know," Hakeem said, rubbing his hand gently across Darcy's face.

"Hakeem! *Now!*"

"Goodbye, Darcy."

"Goodbye, Hakeem."

Chapter 7

Darcy spent the rest of the day feeling dazed. She sat in the living room flipping TV channels and was startled when Jamee confronted her.

"What's wrong with you? You look like you just went to a funeral," Jamee asked.

"Thanks," Darcy replied, getting up and walking out of the room. She did not want to speak to anyone.

Later that afternoon, Jamee announced that she was going shopping with Mom. "Do you want to come with us?" Mom asked.

"No, I'll stay with Grandma," Darcy said, glad to hear the news. As soon as they left, she went into Grandma's room and sat in the chair next to her bed. Darcy wanted to tell her grandmother about what had happened recently, though Grandma seemed unusually tired.

"Hakeem's gone, Grandma," she said, uncertain whether her grandmother was able to listen to her.

"I just need to rest, Angelcake," Grandma said softly, her eyes barely opening.

Listening to Grandma's shallow breathing, Darcy felt more alone than ever. She was wondering whether Hakeem was thinking about her when she heard a loud knock at the front door. Quickly, she walked to the door and peered through the eyehole. Standing on the step in a white tank top and jeans was Brian.

"Brian, what are you doing here?" she asked, opening the door.

"I was in the neighborhood, so I figured I'd stop by to see if you were home," Brian said, sliding his hands into his pockets.

"I'm watching my grandmother. She's not feeling so well today," Darcy explained. As she spoke, Darcy realized she was wearing a beat-up pair of jeans. She felt uncomfortable looking so sloppy in front of Brian.

"Oh, I didn't realize this was a bad

time. Maybe I can come over some other time."

"No, it's all right. I'm glad you stopped by," Darcy said, glancing back toward Grandma's room.

"Are you okay?" Brian asked. "I mean, after your breakup and everything."

Darcy did not know what to say. She felt strange telling Brian about Hakeem, but she wanted to talk to someone, and Brian always seemed so nice.

"Hakeem moved away today, and I don't think I'm going to see him again. I mean, I know we broke up and all, but it's still sad, you know?" she said, surprised at her honesty.

"You wanna talk about it?" he said, moving closer.

Looking into his eyes, Darcy felt the same awkwardness she felt at the beach, but she did not want him to leave. "Sure," she said. "Come on in."

Darcy led Brian into the living room, and they sat on the couch together. Quickly, Darcy recounted the events of the past weeks, including her breakup with Hakeem and their final goodbye.

"I know this isn't easy for you, but you gotta keep one thing in mind,

Darcy," Brian said. "You can't stop livin' through all this. Just 'cause he's gone don't mean you gotta lock yourself in your house all summer. That wouldn't be right. Besides, who knows what you might miss out on." As Brian spoke, he put his arm around Darcy's shoulder. "I mean it," he said.

"Thanks, Brian," Darcy said, surprised at how his advice seemed like what Tarah said weeks ago. *Maybe they're right,* she thought to herself, *but should I just forget about Hakeem?*

"I was hoping we'd have some time together 'cause I wanted to give you something," Brian said, reaching into his pocket. He pulled out a small velvet box and handed it to her. Speechless, Darcy opened the box. Inside was a sparkling gold chain.

"Brian!" Darcy exclaimed. The necklace shimmered like liquid fire.

"After our day on the beach, I saw this and thought it would look nice on you."

"Thank you, Brian, but I can't accept this. It's too much."

"It was nothing," Brian added. As Darcy gaped at the necklace, Brian reached down, picked it up, and placed it gently around her neck. For an instant, both his arms rested on her shoulders, and his face moved to within several inches of hers. She could smell his cologne and feel his breath on her face. Her heart raced as his fingers worked to snap the clasp. "There," he said proudly, pulling away from her. "It looks great on you."

"You shouldn't have done this."

"Angelcake," came Grandma's hoarse voice from her bedroom down the hallway. Brian jerked, startled at the sound.

"That's just my grandmother," Darcy explained, getting up from the sofa. "Coming, Grandma," she yelled.

"Well, I should get going so you can be with her," Brian said, standing up and walking toward the door. "Just remember what I told you. I won't be happy if you hide in your house all summer."

Brian walked out the front door, and Darcy was left standing in the living room alone, her fingers resting on the gold necklace draped around her throat.

"Angelcake," Grandma yelled again.

"What is it, Grandma?" Darcy asked as she entered the room.

"Was there a stranger in the house?" she asked, her frail voice wavering.

"No, Grandma, just a friend of mine." Darcy sat next to her, and watched as Grandma gradually calmed down and drifted off to sleep again.

Running the gold necklace between her fingers, Darcy wondered about her conversation with Brian. One thing he said echoed softly in her mind.

"I won't be happy if you hide in your house all summer."

The next day, Tarah and Cooper came over unannounced.

"Surprise!" Tarah greeted Darcy as she opened the door. "We're takin' you out today, and we won't take no for an answer."

"Yeah," Cooper chimed in, "you don't have a choice, kid. You're comin' with us."

"But I wasn't expecting you," Darcy replied.

"Of course you weren't," Tarah replied. "That's why it's a surprise. Me and Coop are takin' you to a movie, and then out for burgers."

"Yeah, we're gonna go see that new scary movie called *Head Count*. It's about a dude who keeps people's heads in his basement," Cooper said, chuckling.

"You guys," Darcy explained, "I really appreciate what you're trying to do for me, but I have to work today."

"Can't you cancel, girl?" Tarah asked. "Do you want me to call out sick for you?"

"No, I can't do that. I already missed a week because of exams. Liselle is counting on me. Why don't we make it for another day this week, maybe Thursday?"

"I don't know if I can wait that long to see this movie," Cooper replied.

"Well then, we'll see a different one," Darcy said. "I don't really like scary movies that much anyway."

"There she goes again makin' everythin' serious," Cooper teased. "You do know they're fake, right? Like them wrestlers on TV. It's all fake. They don't mean nothin'."

"Okay, girl," Tarah said, ignoring Cooper. "We'll make it Thursday. By the way, did you see a certain someone before he left yesterday?"

Darcy nodded. "We said goodbye, and I think we'll still be friends."

"Of course y'all will be. Just give it some time, that's all." Tarah said with a smile, glancing at Cooper. "Well, we gotta go, Darcy, but I'll call you later."

Darcy watched Tarah and Cooper head back down the walkway. She could not help but feel a touch of jealousy as the two of them left together. Even though they always teased each other, Darcy could tell that Cooper and Tarah had something really special. Looking down at her new necklace, which she had slipped under her shirt, Darcy wondered if she would ever be as lucky as the two of them.

Darcy arrived at the Masons' at the usual time. "Come in, Darcy," Liselle said as she opened the door. "I'm actually on time today, so I have a few minutes to talk."

Darcy sat next to Liselle on the sofa. Kelena was in her playpen giggling and clapping. Liselle looked over at her daughter and smiled proudly. "She hardly ever cries," she said. "She'd rather laugh and smile."

"Kelena is the happiest baby I've ever seen," Darcy said, waving at the baby. "She never gives me any trouble at all."

Darcy noticed that Liselle seemed a bit tense, as if she had something to say, but did not know how to say it.

"How are you doing?" Liselle asked after a brief pause. "Brian told me your school year is over, and I remember you saying that your boyfriend would leave right after school ended."

Darcy wondered why Liselle was so curious about her boyfriend. "Actually, he left yesterday morning," she said.

"I'm sorry," Liselle sighed, leaning toward Darcy. "Are you okay?"

"I think so," Darcy replied slowly. "We broke up about a week ago, and at first things were really bad, but we talked yesterday, and I think we can be friends. Everybody keeps telling me not to stop my life over it. Actually, Brian has been very sweet to me since all this started."

Liselle nodded. "You just take your time. It's hard when you lose someone you care about. Believe me, I know. If you need anything, just page me at school," Liselle said before leaving and locking the door behind her.

After Liselle left, Kelena took a nap, and Darcy sat in the quiet apartment. For a while, she looked through a few magazines she found on the coffee table. Then she decided to explore the Masons' apartment. Walking down the short hallway,

Darcy examined the pictures of Kelena that were on the walls. At the end of the hall, Darcy noticed one door was closed. It had to be Brian's bedroom, since Kelena and Liselle slept together. Staring at the closed door, Darcy was filled with curiosity. What was Brian's room like? she wondered.

Darcy knew she should not snoop. But what harm could she do by peeking into a room? Besides, she wasn't going to take anything. After checking to make sure Kelena was sound asleep, Darcy returned to the end of the hallway and grabbed the cold metal doorknob. She would just take one peek and close the door, she promised herself.

Turning her wrist slowly, Darcy discovered the doorknob would not budge. Brian's door was locked.

Going back to the living room, Darcy felt guilty for trying to open Brian's bedroom door. But she also felt curious. *Why would Brian lock his own room?*

Throughout the evening, Darcy wondered about Brian and why Liselle had acted so peculiar whenever his name was mentioned. When Liselle returned hours later, Darcy wanted to ask her about Brian. But Liselle seemed tired and uninterested in talking, so Darcy kept her thoughts to herself.

Darcy and Jamee spent most of Wednesday morning doing chores around the house. Mom and Dad were both working. Darcy was reaching up to dust a high shelf when Jamee startled her.

"Where'd you get that necklace?" Jamee asked, pointing to the gold chain now draped outside Darcy's black T-shirt. "I know Hakeem didn't buy you that."

"Brian bought it for me," Darcy admitted reluctantly. So far, nobody else seemed to notice the chain.

"Ooooh," Jamee exclaimed, getting a closer look. "I bet that was really expensive. What's going on between you two, anyway?"

"Jamee, it's a long story, and to tell you the truth, I don't know," she said.

"Did you tell Hakeem?"

"No," Darcy answered quickly. "Besides, things between me and Hakeem got real complicated right before he left."

"Complicated?" Jamee seemed confused. "What was so complicated? Did you guys break up or somethin'?"

Darcy was about to reply when the

doorbell rang. Jamee rushed to answer it.

"Is Darcy home?" said the person at the door.

"You must be Brian," Jamee said, opening the door. "I'm Jamee, Darcy's sister." Watching the way Jamee smiled, Darcy knew her sister thought Brian was handsome.

"Hi, Brian!" Darcy exclaimed, stepping in front of Jamee. "What are you doing here?"

"Hey, Darcy," Brian smiled "I came by to see if you wanted to take a ride down to the park. I don't have to work until 6:00, and I thought it'd be nice to hang out for a few hours."

Darcy was thrilled to see Brian, but she knew she had told Mom and Dad that she would stay home and keep an eye on Grandma today. "Oh, Brian, I can't," Darcy began, "It sounds great, but I'm sitting with my Grandma today and—"

"You can go, Darcy," Jamee interrupted. "Our chores are done. I can stay here with Grandma. She'll probably sleep through the rest of the day anyway."

"I don't know, Jamee," Darcy said, thinking about her grandmother's weariness and her recent spells of crankiness. "I told Mom and Dad that I would be here too. I'm not sure I should leave you alone, you know, with Grandma the way she is."

"I'm not a baby," Jamee snapped. "I'm only two years younger than you, Darcy. Besides, I've stayed with her by myself before."

"Looks like your li'l sis will be fine," Brian said, giving Jamee a wink.

For an instant, Darcy debated whether she should stay home. But Jamee's wide smile and Brian's playful grin convinced her it would be okay to leave for a few hours. Besides, Jamee had watched Grandma by herself before.

"Okay," Darcy said, beaming. "I'll go. But I won't be gone long, Jamee."

"Have fun, Darce," Jamee smiled. "And remember, you owe me one."

Brian and Darcy drove over to Delancey Park on the other side of the neighborhood. The park was not far from Lincoln High School, and it was in much better shape than the parks around Bluford. While Darcy's neighborhood park was littered with beer bottles, trash bags, and graffiti, Delancey was clean. Even the benches were in good shape, unlike the broken ones Darcy was used to.

"Neighbors patrol this park almost every night," Brian said as they walked under a massive oak tree. "All of us on the Lincoln football team used to help clean it too."

The mention of Lincoln High School reminded Darcy of the rumor she had heard about Brian being kicked out of school, which made her more and more curious about him. Was the rumor true? Why was his relationship with his sister strained? She was just about to ask him when Brian reached down and gently took her hand.

Darcy's heart raced as Brian's strong fingers slipped between hers. She could feel her pulse pounding in her neck so loudly she wondered whether Brian could hear it. For an instant, she was speechless. Rather than try to speak, she walked with him in awkward silence.

"I really like spending time with you," Brian said, squeezing her hand gently.

"Me too," Darcy mumbled, her voice barely a whisper. She felt as if she was dreaming, as if Brian, the sunny park, and the touch of his hand were imaginary. Even her own words seemed part

of the dream. But as she looked down at her hand and then up at Brian, she knew everything was real, and she was thrilled. For the rest of the afternoon, Darcy walked hand-in-hand with Brian and talked quietly about music they listened to, places they'd like to go, and plans they had for the coming summer.

When they finally returned to the car, Brian drove back to his apartment so he could get ready for work. Darcy decided to join him, figuring she could talk to Liselle while he was getting ready. But when Brian opened the door to the darkened apartment, Darcy knew immediately that Liselle and Kelena were not home. For a second, she felt nervous to be so alone with Brian. She had never been alone at home with any boy, not even Hakeem. She knew her parents would get upset if they found out she was with an older guy in an empty apartment.

"I'll just be a few minutes," Brian said as he went into his bedroom to get changed. In the brief instant that his bedroom door was opened, Darcy saw what appeared to be several large trophies on a dark wooden dresser. At one point, Brian reappeared to get something out of the bathroom. When Darcy turned to look at him, he was shirtless, and his broad dark back formed a perfect V down to his waist. Darcy blushed and turned away immediately, but the image stayed in her mind like a vivid photograph.

After a few minutes, Brian returned fully dressed in his guard uniform. "Ready to go?" he asked with a smile.

Darcy nodded, and just as she was about to walk out the door, Brian put his hand on her waist and turned her toward him.

"I had a really good time today," he said.

"So did I," Darcy replied, still embarrassed about seeing him shirtless.

"I hope we can see more of each other this summer," he added, staring into her eyes.

Again, Darcy felt like she was dreaming, as if her feet were not touching the floor. As she looked at him, his face came closer to hers, and though she was nervous, she did not turn away. In an instant, his lips were touching hers, and her heart pounded so much she felt her chest might explode.

The kiss lasted a few seconds, and Darcy closed her eyes until Brian slowly pulled away. As they separated, Darcy felt a whirlwind of confusion. She knew so little about Brian, and things were happening so fast. Yet, as she looked into his almond-colored eyes, she knew she did not want to stop seeing him.

Together Brian and Darcy left the apartment and got into his car. In a minute, the Toyota stopped in front of her house, and Darcy stepped out.

"I'll call you," Brian said with a smile. "Thanks for coming to the park with me."

"Bye, Brian," Darcy waved as the Toyota pulled away. In the distance, she heard the wail of a far-off siren. Walking up the path to her front door, Darcy thought about her day with Brian and whether she should tell Tarah about him.

As she reached the top step to her house, Darcy heard the howl of the siren grow louder. Glancing toward the sound, she spotted an ambulance turning the corner onto her street. The ambulance darted around several parked cars and came to a screeching stop in front of her house.

"Did you call an ambulance?" the driver yelled.

Suddenly, Darcy heard the door behind her open.

"She's in here! She won't wake up. Hurry!" Jamee yelled.

Chapter 8

"Oh my God!" Darcy cried. "What happened?!"

Jamee wrapped her arms around Darcy's shoulders and began sobbing. "It's Grandma! I couldn't wake her up!" Jamee cried, her voice quivering.

"Where is she?"

Jamee quickly led Darcy and the paramedics into her grandmother's bedroom. Darcy felt like she had been kicked in the stomach when she saw Grandma sprawled on the floor.

Darcy grabbed her sister's hand as the medics hoisted Grandma's limp body onto a stretcher. The girls followed them as they carried Grandma outside.

"Did you call Mom and Dad?" asked Darcy.

"Yeah. Mom's at the hospital, and Dad's on his way there. I called them right after I called 911. Mom said to stay here and wait for them to get back from the hospital. She said one of them would call as soon as they learned something."

After the emergency technicians put Grandma into the ambulance, one of them strapped a plastic mask across her face.

"She's still breathing," yelled a paramedic. Quickly, the driver jumped into the ambulance and slammed the door. Within seconds, the vehicle was screeching down the street towards the hospital, lights flashing.

Back inside the house, Jamee explained she had gone into Grandma's room and found her lying on the floor unconscious. "I tried to wake her, but nothing happened," she said. "That's when I called 911."

Darcy felt a twisting feeling in her stomach. She imagined the horror Jamee must have felt when she discovered Grandma on the floor. She was angry at herself for not being home when Grandma passed out.

"This might not have happened if I had stayed here," Darcy said. "I shouldn't have left you two alone. I should've been here."

"There's nothing you could have done," Jamee insisted. "I just hope she's gonna be all right."

Darcy sat on the couch, unable to push the image of her unconscious grandmother from her mind. She wanted to call the hospital, but she was afraid her parents might try to contact her while she was on the phone. Part of her wanted to call Hakeem. He had always been there whenever she had problems in the family. Now he was hundreds of miles away, and even if he were nearby, she could not imagine calling him, especially after what happened with Brian.

The evening wore on slowly, and with each passing minute, Darcy feared more and more for Grandma. Finally, she heard a car pull into the driveway. Darcy trembled as her father walked up the front steps, the sound of his feet heavy and slow.

"How's Grandma?" Darcy asked as soon as he opened the door.

"She's doing all right," Dad said, "but she gave us a good scare."

"What happened?" Jamee asked.

"She must have tried to get out of bed by herself," Dad replied, joining his daughters on the sofa. "She probably lost her balance and fell on the floor. When she went down, she must have hit her head on the bed frame. It took her a few hours to come out of it, but she's doing much better. The doctors are keeping her overnight for more observation, and your mother's staying there with her."

"I'm sorry I wasn't here," Darcy cried. "I feel like this is all my fault."

"If anyone is to blame, it's me," Jamee said. "I'm the one who was home. But I thought she was sleeping like she usually does—"

"This is no one's fault," Dad said, putting his arms around both girls. "Your Grandma didn't fall because of you two. You know your grandmother. When she sets her mind on something, nothing is gonna stop her."

"But I should have been here," Darcy insisted. "If I was in the room with her, she wouldn't have fallen." Darcy's father hugged her but said nothing for a moment.

"You girls should get some sleep. Grandma's okay, and there's nothing more we can do tonight," Dad said finally, getting up from the sofa.

Watching him walk slowly down the hallway, Darcy knew she was not about to fall asleep anytime soon. She decided to stay up and wait for her mother to come home from the hospital.

"How is she?" Darcy said when Mom walked in around midnight.

"She's sleeping," Mom said wearily. Her eyes were swollen and glassy. "I came home to get a shower and sleep for an hour or two. Then, I'll go right back and sit with her some more, until I find out what the doctors have to say."

"Can I go with you, Mom?" Darcy asked. "I'd like to sit with her too."

"I don't think that's such a good idea," Mom said as she trudged to her bedroom. "You stay here with Jamee. She needs you right now." A second later, Darcy heard the bedroom door close.

The house became deathly silent, the living room dark except for the ghostly glow of a small night light. Darcy felt more alone than ever.

Darcy tossed and turned throughout the night. Every so often, she glanced at her clock hoping she might fall asleep. The minutes rolled by, but she could not relax. At 1:30, she tried to read a book, but she could not concentrate. At 3:00, she fluffed up her pillow, turned her light on, and looked at old pictures of her grandmother. By 5:00, her eyes were exhausted, but she still was not sleepy.

At sunrise, birds began squawking loudly outside her window, reminding Darcy of Grandma and making her feel even more depressed. So many things had changed so suddenly, she thought. Hakeem was gone. Grandma was in the hospital. And then there was Brian. She still could not believe that only hours earlier she had kissed him in a way she had never kissed Hakeem.

Finally, in midmorning, Darcy fell asleep and dreamed that she was walking along the beach. As she walked, the sand in her dream became soft and deep, and she felt her body sinking. She struggled to free herself, but the sand quickly rose around her until it covered her chest, spilled into her mouth, and began to choke her. Screaming in her dream, Darcy sat upright in her bed. The house was silent.

At noon, Mom called to say that Grandma's condition was improving. "They are planning to send her home tomorrow." Hearing those words, Darcy felt as if a great weight had been removed from her shoulders.

"Grandma's doing better," Darcy announced to Dad and Jamee. "And she'll be coming home tomorrow!"

"Thank goodness!" Jamee exclaimed, relief and happiness in her voice.

Her father nodded thoughtfully several times, but returned to the kitchen.

Darcy was thrilled with the news. She could not wait for Grandma to be home and for their family to return to normal. Leaning back in the living room chair, Darcy thought again about how just twenty-four hours ago she had kissed Brian. It seemed as if that had happened weeks ago, not yesterday.

Darcy wondered what Brian really thought about her. She wanted to call him, but she felt awkward every time she imagined their conversation.

"Hi, Brian, this is Darcy," she'd say. *"Are you for real? Do you really like me, or are you just playing games?"* She knew the questions were silly, but she wanted to know the answers. Part of her wished she could talk to someone about him, and she felt dishonest for keeping Brian a secret from Tarah and her parents. But she was certain they would be angry that

she had kissed a nineteen-year-old, especially so soon after Hakeem left.

"Don't stop living when Hakeem leaves," Tarah had said weeks ago.

Darcy wanted to tell Tarah the truth, that she had not stopped living, that someone new was coming into her life. But she was not sure how serious Brian was, and she also was not sure about herself. She still felt guilty when she thought of Hakeem, but whenever she spent time with Brian, that guilt seemed to dissolve.

Later in the afternoon, Jamee barged into Darcy's room when she was trying to take a nap. "You have a phone call. It's Brian, your new boyfriend," Jamee teased.

"He's not my boyfriend," Darcy blurted.

"Yeah, right," Jamee replied as Darcy rushed for the phone.

"Hello," Darcy said, trying to hide how excited his call made her.

"What's up, baby?" Brian asked.

Darcy hesitated briefly and then explained what had happened to Grandma and how she had been up all night.

"I'm sorry, Darcy," Brian said. "I understand what you're going through. Just take care of your family, and give me a call when things settle down."

"Thanks, Brian," she replied, hoping he would not hang up. She wanted to see him again but felt awkward suggesting they get together. For an instant, there was silence on the phone, and then Brian spoke.

"I really had a good time yesterday," he said.

"Me too. Maybe we can go out again soon," she suggested nervously, surprised at her own words.

"You want to come over for dinner tonight?" Brian asked quickly, his voice rising. "I can order pizza and we can chill. I don't have to be at work until 9:00."

Darcy's heart pounded at Brian's offer. She had not planned to see him so soon, but the thought of spending more time with him was very tempting. For an instant, she wanted to ask whether Liselle and Kelena would be home, but she was afraid it would seem rude or childish. She knew her parents would not let her spend time alone with a boy, especially after dark, but she did not mention that to Brian.

"I can be there at 5:30."

"Cool. I'll see you then, Darcy."

After she hung up, Darcy noticed Jamee staring at her from across the room. She wondered whether her sister had listened to their entire conversation.

"What?" Darcy asked, glaring at her sister.

"I hope you're not planning to go out. Dad's cooking tonight, and he wants us all to sit down and eat together. He's making his roasted chicken," Jamee said.

"That's right," Dad said, walking into the living room with a spatula in his hand. "You girls are gonna love this meal tonight. Your old Dad has really outdone himself this time."

"Isn't that what you *always* say?" Jamee teased.

As much as she wanted to be with her family, Darcy was eager to see Brian again. He made her feel special, and now they had plans to have their first dinner together. Darcy did not want to call him back to cancel. "Guys, I can't eat here tonight," Darcy said.

"Why not?" Dad asked, looking surprised. Jamee's eyes widened.

"I . . . have to babysit," Darcy said, looking at Jamee as she spoke. Jamee's jaw dropped, but she said nothing.

"Tonight? Isn't there somebody else they can get?" Dad asked, looking at Darcy. He did not seem to notice Jamee's reaction.

"No, Daddy, they don't have anybody else."

"Baby, I wanted you to be here for dinner, so we could eat together as a family. We've been through so much this week," he said, pausing for a moment and seeming a bit hurt by Darcy's announcement. "But if you have to go, we'll understand."

"Thanks, Daddy. I won't be late."

"I'll keep a plate hot for you, baby. This is a real nice thing you're doin' for that girl. I hope she appreciates it."

"I'm sure she does," Darcy said, smiling.

"You owe me another one," Jamee said just before Darcy left. "I don't know what's going on with you two, but I've never seen you act this way before, not with Hakeem or anyone."

Jamee's words haunted Darcy as she headed over to the Masons'. At the door of the apartment, Darcy wondered whether she should turn around and go home. She had never lied to her father before, and Hakeem had been gone less than two weeks.

But the thought of seeing Brian lured her. More than anything, Darcy was happy to have someone special in her life, someone who was interested in her, someone who thrilled her with his touch. Her fingers tingled as she knocked on the wooden door of the Masons' apartment.

Brian opened the door seconds later, and Darcy noticed the scent of incense coming from the apartment. The lights in the living room were turned down, and the entire apartment was bathed in a dim amber glow.

Darcy knew instantly that Kelena and Liselle were not home. The small television was on, featuring a music video of a man rapping inside a ring of fire. Glancing at the other side of the room, Darcy noticed two plates on the coffee table. A pizza box was sitting between the plates. "I'm glad you came over," Brian said, turning off the TV. "I'm sorry about what happened to your grandmother."

"Thanks," Darcy said. "She's gonna be okay. The doctors are sending her home tomorrow."

"You must be exhausted," Brian said. "Have a seat." He gestured toward the sofa. "I wanted you to relax, so I tried to make things as nice as possible." He lit a small white candle on the coffee table, and then sat next to her. Darcy's heart began to race. She had been alone with Brian before, but never *this* alone.

"I can't believe I'm here alone with you. I told my dad I'm babysitting," Darcy admitted, shaking her head. She kept her hands on her lap so Brian would not notice how much they trembled. "Where are Liselle and Kelena today?" she asked.

"Oh, they're invited to a friend's for dinner. They won't be home for hours," Brian answered as he got up from the sofa. "You look so tense. I think I know how to relax you." He walked behind the couch where she was sitting and placed his warm hands on the back of her neck. Then he began to gently massage her shoulders.

"I like you a lot, Darcy," Brian confessed. "I've liked you since the first day you came over to meet Kelena. I just kept hoping one day you'd like me too, and now here you are."

Darcy felt Brian's powerful fingers moving in circles along her shoulders. His touch seemed to push his words deeper into her mind. And though part of her was startled by Brian's confession, another part of her felt entranced by his words.

"Relax," he said, moving his hands more slowly.

Darcy leaned back in the sofa and dropped her head forward so he could massage her more completely. Her eyes were closed, and she felt almost like she was on the beach again, listening to waves break against the shore line.

With her eyes closed, under the steady pressure of his hands, Darcy almost forgot that she had lied to her father, that she was alone with Brian, that she had never done anything like this before with Hakeem or anyone.

Darcy felt Brian's breath against the back of her neck, and she turned towards him. His lips met hers, and as they kissed, a feeling of electricity raced from her lips into her body. She gently placed her arms around his warm neck.

Quickly, Brian leaned across the couch and into Darcy. Kissing her, he squeezed his body closer. She could smell his cologne and feel the thick muscles in his shoulders and back.

Closing her eyes, Darcy imagined she was on the beach walking slowly with her hands entwined with his. Then Brian's face changed, and for an instant, she was walking with Hakeem. Startled, she opened her eyes, and Brian was leaning into her, his lips tight against hers.

Darcy felt as if she was watching herself in a movie. She could see Brian leaning against her, and she could see herself kissing him. But the movie was happening too fast. Brian's kisses, Grandma's illness, Hakeem's departure, the lie to her father—all of it was too fast, and Darcy could not seem to stop it.

Brian's hand snaked down from her shoulder. For an instant, she felt it rest hot against her waist. Then his fingers began tugging at the base of her shirt.

Darcy moved her hand over Brian's fingers to stop them.

"Relax," Brian said, running his other hand along Darcy's face as she stared into his dark eyes. "It's okay." Then he started to kiss her neck.

Closing her eyes again, Darcy felt Brian's hand return to the bottom of her shirt. A second later he was beginning to peel it upward.

"Brian—"

"Just relax," he repeated, an edge to his voice. "Everything's going to be fine."

Again his hand slipped lower, and this time Darcy grabbed it. "Brian, stop it," she insisted.

"There's nothing to be afraid of," Brian said, glaring at her. "Why are you making such a big deal?"

Darcy felt embarrassed under his gaze. She wanted him to stop looking at her, and she felt foolish for getting so upset. Still, Brian was going too far. She was surprised when he started kissing her again.

"Brian!" she yelled, twisting away from him. As she turned, her leg smacked against the edge of the table, knocking the pizza box and plates to the floor.

"What's wrong with you?" Brian yelled, anger in his eyes. He stood over her now, his hands gripping the top of her arms, his pulse pounding in his neck. "You're acting like a baby."

Pain from his grasp shot into her arm. "Brian, let go. You're hurting me!" Struggling to free herself, she knocked a nearby lamp over with her flailing foot. The lamp broke as it hit the floor.

"Let me *go!*" she screamed.

"Calm down!" Brian commanded loudly, shaking her.

Darcy wrestled her left arm free and slapped Brian across the face. "Let me *GO!*" she yelled again. Her hand stung from the impact against Brian's skin, and she watched in horror as his eyes widened in rage. Instantly, Brian's grip tightened, and Darcy found herself unable to break free.

"Brian, *stop!*" Darcy cried, as sharp pains began ripping into her arms like stabbing knives.

Chapter 9

Suddenly, Darcy heard a loud knock at the apartment's front door. Brian turned in surprise.

"Darcy!" cried a familiar voice from the other side of the door. "Are you okay? Let me in!" Darcy recognized her father's voice. Before she could react, the front door smashed inward.

"Daddy!" Darcy yelled. Seeing him, Brian let go of Darcy and took a step away from the couch.

Without a word, Dad charged into the small living room like a speeding freight train. He gripped Brian's neck and thrust his body forward. Caught off guard, Brian barely had a chance to raise his arms before he slammed into the far wall of the living room. The impact of Brian's head against the plaster caused two pictures to crash to the floor.

"Daddy!" Darcy screamed as her father pounced on Brian, seizing his neck again and glaring in anger. Brian's eyes were bright with fear, and sweat glistened on his forehead.

"Did you try and hurt my girl?" Dad growled.

"I didn't mean nothin'. I didn't mean to—"

"Daddy, it was a mistake," Darcy pleaded.

"Don't you say anything, Darcy," her father yelled, still holding Brian by his throat. "I can tell by the looks of things that you didn't come here to babysit. You and I are gonna talk about that in a minute."

Darcy felt her face burn with shame, but she said nothing. Her father turned back towards Brian who suddenly seemed much smaller.

"Now, I don't know what you were thinking, but the next time a girl tells you to back off, you listen. And if you ever mess with my daughter again, it'll be the last mistake you make. You hear me, boy?"

Brian nodded nervously, and Dad pushed him aside in a gesture of contempt and anger.

Darcy ran over to her father and threw her arms around him. "Daddy, I'm sorry," she said.

"C'mon, let's get you home," her father said coldly.

As they walked out of the apartment, Darcy turned back to see Brian. He glared at her and then slammed the apartment door shut. Darcy and her father were in the corridor alone.

"I'm glad I decided to bring dinner to you," her father said angrily, picking up a covered dinner plate left next to the Masons' door. "I felt bad about you having to work while the rest of us were eating. I thought it would be nice surprise if I brought you a hot meal. But when I got to the door, I heard all this yelling and then I heard a crash—"

"Dad, I'm sorry," Darcy repeated, tears welling in her eyes.

"Darcy, I trusted you!" her father yelled as they walked home. "Do you have any idea what could have happened?"

"But Dad, I—"

"I don't want to hear it, Darcy. What you did was *stupid*. I'm so angry right now, I don't even want to look at you. Don't ask me to trust you again, not after this."

Her father stormed off, and Darcy followed, tears streaming down her face. She had never been in this much trouble. And she had never felt more alone.

"I tried to stop Dad," Jamee said later that night. "But he wanted to bring you dinner. I knew it was a bad idea for you to sneak over Brian's. At least for once I'm not the one getting in trouble."

Darcy grunted. She did not even look at Jamee, who was sitting on the opposite side of her bed.

"So what happened anyway?" Jamee asked.

"Look, I don't want to talk about it right now, okay?" Darcy snapped. She could tell that her father had not told Jamee anything about what had taken place at the Masons' apartment. Darcy was grateful that Jamee did not know. Jamee liked to gossip, and Darcy knew that all of Bluford would talk about how her father beat up Brian if her sister got the story.

"Sorry," Jamee said, getting up from the bed. "Don't worry, Darcy. Dad doesn't stay angry long. I should know."

Darcy closed her bedroom door after Jamee left. In the quiet of her bedroom, she rubbed the dark bruise where Brian had gripped her arm. She could not believe what had happened just hours earlier, and she did not know what to think about Brian.

Part of her feared him. He should have stopped touching her when she asked him to. Of this, Darcy was certain. But she was not convinced he was totally to blame. Perhaps he did not understand how serious she was when she told him to stop. Or maybe she should have talked to him before they got so physical or before she agreed to be alone with him. Darcy shuddered as a wave of guilt, shame, and confusion washed over her.

Lying in her bed, Darcy remembered how hard she fought Brian and how frightened she had been. No matter what she should have done, Darcy concluded, Brian should not have behaved so aggressively. He was the real guilty party. There was no excuse for him to ignore her wishes or act so violently.

In twisted dreams hours later, Darcy relived the experience over and over again, grateful each time that she woke up in her own bed and that her father had arrived when he did.

The next morning, Darcy woke up in pain, her wrists and arms aching from the struggle with Brian. Listening to the silence of the gray morning, Darcy wondered where her father was and whether he had told her mother what happened. She was afraid to face them. She doubted if they would ever trust her again.

Pulling the blankets up over her head, Darcy wished she could just go to sleep and not have to face her parents, Jamee, or anyone. Then she heard a knock on her door.

"Darcy, wake up. Liselle Mason's on the phone," Jamee said.

Darcy winced at the sound of Jamee's voice. The last thing she wanted to do was talk to Liselle. "Can't you tell her I'll call her back?" Darcy asked.

"No, she says it's important."

Darcy reluctantly got out of bed. "Are Mom and Dad here?" she asked before opening her bedroom door.

"No, they went to get Grandma. They won't be back until this afternoon."

Relieved, Darcy walked out into the hallway and grabbed the phone "Hi, Liselle."

"Darcy, I'm sorry this is such short

notice, but I need to get some extra studying done, and I wanted to know if you could babysit this afternoon."

Darcy took a deep breath. Brian must not have told his sister about what had happened. For an instant, Darcy hesitated, thinking of what to say. "Liselle, I . . . won't be able to babysit Kelena anymore."

"What?" Liselle asked, her voice rising in surprise. "Why not?"

Darcy looked over her shoulder to make sure Jamee was not listening. Lowering her voice, she spoke just above a whisper. "Look, Liselle, I just can't do it, okay."

"Darcy, what's wrong? Did I do something?"

"It's not you," Darcy paused debating whether to tell the truth. "It's . . . Brian."

"What did *he* do?" Liselle asked, anger rising in her voice. "I knew he was going to do something wrong. He had his eye on you since day one. "

"What do you mean?"

Liselle paused for a second. "Brian's a player, Darcy. He's a smooth talker, and he's always chasin' a pretty face and a nice body. Girls fall for it, too. They're always callin' him on his beeper. He's been a dog for years, though he won't admit it. I guess I thought you'd be be smart enough to see through his act."

Darcy's face burned with anger and shame. "Yeah, well I guess you were wrong."

"I've been trying to get him to change his ways since he lost his football scholarship."

"He played college football?" Darcy asked, surprised.

"Division One, for a while. He hurt his knee at the end of his first year. Then he started gettin' into trouble, and they kicked him out. That's why he never told you about it. He probably never told you about the baby he fathered either. Because of him, there's some poor girl out there right just like me tryin' to raise a child without a father. Like I said, I've been tryin' to get him to straighten up his act, but he don't listen to nobody," Liselle said bitterly. "So tell me what happened."

"Look, it was nothing serious." Darcy said, trying to hide the anger she felt toward Brian. "But I just can't babysit anymore."

For several seconds, Liselle remained quiet. Darcy knew she was waiting to hear her describe what had happened with Brian. But Darcy was not about to share her experiences with Liselle, especially with Jamee nearby.

"I understand," Liselle responded finally with a sigh. "Anyway, I'm beginnin' to add up two and two. I'll bet this has somethin' to do with the mess I found in the apartment when I came home last night. Brian told me some of his friends came over and got a little wild, but now I see it was somethin' else, something worse. I'm sorry, Darcy."

Darcy heard frustration and sadness in Liselle's voice. And she felt bad about leaving Liselle without a babysitter. Still, as she hung up, she knew there was no way she would spend another second in the Mason apartment.

The silence in the living room seemed deafening. Liselle's words ricocheted through her mind, filling her with rage. She had been fooled, she realized. Brian had lured her with his kind words. It had all been an act.

Remembering her actions over the past weeks drove spikes of guilt into Darcy's heart, guilt for spending time away from Grandma, for lying to her family, for hiding the truth from her friends.

Ashamed of her behavior, Darcy also felt violated, as if Brian had robbed her of something precious—trust.

Several hours later, Darcy's parents returned home with Grandma. Carefully, Dad pushed the wheelchair through the front door and then directly into the far bedroom. Darcy immediately rushed to hug her grandmother, but he cautioned her.

"She needs her rest, Darcy."

"I thought she was better," Jamee replied.

"She is," Mom explained, carrying several bags in from the car. "She's just tired, that's all."

Mom looked ten years older than the last time Darcy saw her. Her eyes were red and puffy, and deep lines marked her brow. Darcy did not know if her parents had discussed what happened with Brian, but for now everyone seemed distracted by Grandma. Looking at her, she understood why.

Grandma seemed more frail than Darcy had ever seen her. In the two days at the hospital, Grandma appeared to have shriveled inside herself. Deep purple bruises marked her arm where IV needles had been injected.

When Dad emerged from the bedroom, he was out of breath and looking tired. "She's still feeling a little under the weather. After a few days of rest, she'll be better," he said.

"But, she's okay, right?" Darcy asked nervously.

Dad walked over and sat on the sofa. "Grandma needs her sleep so she can get strong again. That fall took a lot out of her. But her spirit is strong. She'll be back on her feet again. It'll just take some time," Dad explained. But as he spoke, Darcy noticed he did not make eye contact with her. "The doctors say it's okay for her to sleep as much as she does, but we gotta make sure she eats. Aside from that, there's no medicine for what's goin' on with Grandma except time and love." Mom wiped tears from her eyes several times while Dad talked.

Despite her father's hopeful words, Darcy sensed what was happening. *Grandma might not get better,* she thought. It seemed like only yesterday when Grandma sang in the church choir every Sunday morning, her voice booming songs about rising to Heaven and going home. Now maybe it was her turn.

Or maybe Grandma would bounce back again as she had done many times before. Perhaps even tomorrow Grandma would wake up and tell old stories from her childhood. Then her eyes would twinkle again as she recounted memories of growing up in the South, her courtship with Grandpa, and the time Darcy's mother was born.

Even though she had heard the stories before, Darcy wanted to hear them again. She wished they would never stop. Silently, Darcy prayed she would see Grandma's eyes sparkle again.

Later that evening, Darcy sat alone at the kitchen table. Midway through the meal, her parents walked into the room and looked at her. Darcy braced herself as they sat at the table next to her.

"Your father and I talked about what happened yesterday," Mom said sternly. "What were you thinking, girl?! I cannot believe a daughter of mine would lie to her parents. Especially while her own grandmother's in the hospital!"

"Mom, it was a mistake," Darcy pleaded.

"You're damn right it's a mistake!"

"All right, Mattie—"

"You stay out of this, Carl," Mom said firmly. "Darcy, who you do think you are running around with some boy who ain't even in high school? And going to his apartment! You are lucky your father came in when he did!"

"I know, Mom."

"Shut your mouth! You obviously don't know or you wouldn't have been there. I trusted you! What kind of example are you showing your sister?"

"You can still trust me."

"Darcy Wills, it will be a long time before I trust you again. I am so upset. How could you do such a thing? And with Grandma being so sick?" Darcy's mother whispered the last words as if Grandma was listening in the other room.

Darcy shrugged her shoulders. Tears welled in her eyes. "I'm sorry."

"Oh, you'll be sorry. You're grounded for a month. You hear me?"

Darcy nodded, and her mother stormed off. Dad followed her, but as he left he gently patted Darcy's back. "It's gonna be okay," he whispered.

Ashamed, Darcy walked into her room, closed the door, and wept.

Chapter 10

Late that night, Darcy was unable to sleep. Her mother's words haunted her like a nightmare from which she could not awaken. Never had Mom been so angry at her. Each time she shut her eyes, Darcy could see Mom's angry face staring back at her.

"How could you do such a thing?" Mom's words echoed over and over in Darcy's mind. Worse than Mom's anger was the fact that Darcy knew what Mom said was true. She was wrong to leave Grandma, and she was wrong to lie to her father. Darcy felt she had done everything wrong since Hakeem left.

"What were you thinking?" Darcy could almost hear Mom yelling in the silence of her bedroom. She wanted to reply to her mother, to have a good excuse to tell her, but she was not sure why

things had gone so wrong so quickly.

"I'm sorry," Darcy said aloud in the darkness. But the words did not make her feel better. Unable to relax, Darcy crept quietly out of her bedroom and went toward Grandma's room.

As a child, whenever she was upset, Darcy would talk to her grandmother. Years ago, when Darcy's father first abandoned them, Grandma held the family together. Countless times, Darcy found comfort in her grandmother's arms. But now, as Darcy sat in the old wooden chair next to Grandma's bed, it seemed those arms would be unable to help.

"I'm sorry, Grandma," Darcy whispered. "I'm sorry I wasn't here when you needed me."

All Darcy heard in reply was the sound of her grandmother's labored breathing, but it did not matter. Being next to Grandma made her feel better. Sitting in the darkness, Darcy could not stop the flood of words pushing to escape her.

"I've really messed up, Grandma," Darcy said, and then she told her grandmother what had happened over the past weeks. She mentioned the loss of Hakeem and how Brian had distracted

her from her sadness. Darcy also confessed how she liked Brian and that he
helped her forget about Grandma's sickness and Hakeem's absence. She even
admitted how Brian had fooled her and
how she had lied to Dad in order to see
him. And when she finished, Darcy told
Grandma about the shame she felt and
how angry she was for having made
such mistakes.

"I let them all down. Every person I
love, I let down, and I don't know how
I'm gonna make it right," Darcy continued. "I am so sorry, Grandma." Darcy
sobbed and lowered her head down into
her grandmother's lap.

As she wept, Darcy felt Grandma's
shoulder start to move. Slowly the old
woman raised her arm and rested her
hand gently against the side of Darcy's
face.

"Its okay, Angelcake," Grandma
whispered, softly stroking Darcy's hair.
Hot tears streamed from Darcy's eyes.
She had not expected her grandmother
to be awake. And now, just as she had
done so many times before, Grandma
comforted her.

After a few minutes, Grandma's hand
returned to her side, and she drifted off

to sleep again, her breathing heavy and labored.

Careful not to make a sound, Darcy wiped her eyes and pulled a blanket over Grandma's shoulder. As she sat back in the chair, Darcy noticed her mother standing in the doorway. In the dim glow of the hallway night light, Darcy could see a glint of moisture in her eyes.

"Mom?" Darcy whispered, getting up.

Without a word, Darcy's mother reached her arms out and embraced her daughter.

"I'm sorry, Mom," Darcy said, feeling her mother's arms around her.

"I know, baby. I know. I'm sorry too." As her mother spoke, she brushed the tears from Darcy's eyes in the same way Grandma once did. "You need to get some sleep," she added.

Weary from crying and from the events of the past month, Darcy nodded, drifted to her bedroom, and sank into her bed. Within minutes, she was overtaken by a deep, heavy sleep.

"Carl! Girls! Come quickly!" Mom's voice cried.

Darcy opened her eyes and suspected immediately that something was wrong with Grandma. She leaped out of bed and rushed down the hallway to Grandma's bedroom.

Jamee and her parents were already in the room when Darcy arrived. They were standing around Grandma's bed in silence. Grandma lay motionless before them, her shrunken body bathed in a shaft of morning sunlight that filled the room with a golden glow. A smile was on Grandma's face and her eyes were closed.

"She's gone," Dad said, his eyes moist. "She came here to be with us one last time, and now she's in a better place."

Darcy's mother sobbed, and Darcy and Jamee rushed to hug her. "She told me last night that she was going home," Mom said, putting her arms around her daughters. "I guess she knew."

Darcy began to cry uncontrollably, and tears poured freely from her eyes, an endless stream of love and sorrow for her lost grandmother. Then Jamee hugged her, and Dad and Mom joined them both. Together the family held each other in a long embrace, one in which tears and touch spoke what words could not.

Behind them, the sun continued to brighten. For several long moments, the room was silent except for the occasional sound of muffled sobs.

Mom wiped her eyes, knelt over to kiss her mother on the cheek, then turned to look at her family. "This was how she always wanted it," Mom said, in a soft voice. "With her family, with all of us together."

Darcy nodded. Dad looked toward the window, tears still in his eyes. "Do you see that?" he asked excitedly. "Do y'all see it?"

A small yellow bird had perched on Grandma's windowsill. It began to chirp, and its song merged with that of other birds in the backyard. Darcy had never heard the birds sing more beautifully.

"They're singing for Grandma," Jamee said. "They're singing for her."

The funeral was held at Holy Faith Church, which sat at the corner of a busy neighborhood street. On the front steps of the church, Darcy and her family greeted mourners who had come to pay their respects to her grandmother.

Darcy was surprised at the large turnout that came to honor Grandma. In the crowd were many people Darcy had not seen since childhood, and some whom she had never met.

Tarah and Cooper arrived just before the service was about to start. Tarah was wearing a long black dress, and Cooper a fine-looking black suit. Darcy was honored to see them so dressed up, and grateful they came to support her and her family.

"I'm so glad you guys made it," she said, wrapping her arms around Tarah, and then around Cooper.

"Girl, of course we would," Tarah said warmly. "We would've been here earlier if somebody knew how to tie a tie."

"Hey," Cooper whispered, "don't blame it on me, Miss I-Need-To-Borrow-My-Mama's-Dress."

Darcy smiled for the first time in days. "It doesn't matter what you wear," she said. "I'm just glad you're here." As she spoke, the church bells rang, signaling the start of the service.

Tarah and Cooper were ushered into the church, and Darcy's parents and sister walked together into the building. As Darcy turned to follow them in, she heard hurried footsteps on the sidewalk behind her. She looked back and saw Brisana Meeks rushing up the walkway.

"I'm sorry about your grandmother," Brisana said, out of breath.

Even though they had not always gotten along, Darcy was grateful Brisana came to support her. It seemed as if years had passed since the school year ended and they had last spoken. Darcy remembered how she had yelled when Brisana tried to warn her about Brian Mason. Now Darcy knew Brisana had been right. She knew she owed her old friend an apology, but that would come at another time.

"Thanks for being here for me, Brisana," Darcy said.

The sight of Grandma's shiny silver coffin sitting in the front of the church stunned her. It took all Darcy's effort just to steady herself so she could join her family in the front pew.

At the end of the service, Reverend Simmons, himself a friend of Grandma's, invited people to say a few words about her. Darcy glanced at her family and saw that Mom, Jamee and Aunt Charlotte were too grief-stricken to speak, and Dad's head was hung low in mourning.

Unsure of what she would say, Darcy felt compelled to pay a tribute to Grandma. Nervously, she got up from the pew and took a step into the center aisle. The church sat quietly as she approached the platform.

She stood just a few feet from her grandmother's open coffin, and she felt her eyes drawn to Grandma as she spoke. Years of memories, of happy and sad times with Grandma flashed through her mind. Leaning in close to the microphone, Darcy closed her eyes and began to speak.

"When I think of things to say about my Grandma, no words seem good enough to describe her," Darcy began. "Years ago, when my parents split up, Grandma was the one who held us together. When my mother struggled to support us by herself, Grandma was the one that made sure we ate dinner and got our homework done. Whenever I needed someone to talk to, Grandma was always there for me. She taught me to believe in myself. And whenever I made a mistake, she was there to catch me." Darcy inhaled and fought back tears.

"I've made some mistakes lately, mistakes that have hurt my family and my friends." As she spoke, Darcy glanced at her family, Cooper, Tarah, and Brisana. Then she turned to the crowd in the church, who seemed to be hanging on her every word. She noticed a few late-comers enter and sit in the empty back pews. Holding back her tears, Darcy took a deep breath and continued.

"But Grandma taught me that love is greater than any mistakes we make. She showed me through her love that families can come back together, that love is sometimes hard work, but it pays off. I don't have Grandma's lap to cry on anymore, but her lessons, her love, and her spirit are with me. Grandma used to say that God sends people into your life to teach you something, and when they go, it's your turn to teach the lesson to others. I know I will use what Grandma taught me to help others. Each time I do, I know Grandma will be smiling. And I know she is smiling down on us all right now."

Darcy stepped down from the podium and returned to her seat. Her mother hugged her as she sat down, and Darcy felt that her grandmother was watching over them. Even in death, Grandma helped the family heal and grow closer.

When Reverend Simmons concluded the service, Darcy and her family led the funeral procession out of the church.

As she stepped outside, Darcy looked into the bright blue sky and heard birds singing. For a moment, a wave of sorrow washed over her, and she wished Grandma was there to hear the song. But another part of her felt Grandma was there. It was *her* song.

Then Darcy noticed a familiar-looking young man making his way through the crowd. Her knees felt weak as he approached, and without a word, she threw her arms around him.

"Hakeem! I can't believe you're here!" Darcy exclaimed. "How—"

"Tarah called and told me what happened, and I wanted to be here for you, Darcy," Hakeem explained. "My uncle paid for my plane ticket. I'll have to work it off this summer, but it's okay because I have nothing else to do in Detroit," he joked, pausing briefly. "Darcy, there was no way I wouldn't be here for you. I'm just sorry I was late."

"No, Hakeem," Darcy replied, wiping her eyes. "You were right on time."

Hakeem smiled, and Darcy led him slowly away from the church. "You look different," he said as they walked.

"I *am* different," Darcy replied.

Those words were among the truest

Darcy had ever spoken. So much had happened since Hakeem left. So many things had changed. In the past month, Darcy had been completely transformed. She had grown and learned lessons which would forever shape her life.

Her experiences taught her what was timeless and unchanging, lessons of family, of loyalty, of friendship. Darcy would never be the same. Of this she was certain. But looking into Hakeem's kind, dark eyes, she knew there was no way of explaining it all to him or anyone else right now.

Instead, she took a deep breath, said a silent prayer, and grabbed Hakeem's hand.

Amidst a symphony of bird song and church bells, they walked together in silence, their warm fingers gently entwined.

Find out what happens next at

BLUFORD HIGH

Blood Is Thicker

Hakeem Randall can't take it anymore. First he learns that his father is sick and his parents can no longer afford their home. Then he must leave his friends at Bluford High and move to his uncle's house in faraway Detroit. Things go from bad to worse when Hakeem is forced to share a small bedroom with his moody and secretive cousin, Savon. Once childhood friends, the two quickly become enemies. Now they are ready to go to war with each other, and the outcome of the battle promises to change their lives forever.

Turn the page for a special sneak preview. . . .

"Goodbye, Darcy," Hakeem Randall said, gently letting go of Darcy Wills, his girlfriend for the past year. The tears in her eyes were like daggers slicing deep into his heart.

"Goodbye, Hakeem."

He watched her walk down the short driveway. If there was anything he could do to stop his family from moving away, he would have done it. But the decision was out of his hands.

Squinting under the Monday morning sun, Hakeem felt like someone had wrapped him in a heavy blanket of gloom. He wouldn't see Darcy again this summer. Maybe not ever. And in just a matter of hours, his old friends at Bluford High School and his home in southern California would be thousands of miles away.

"I'm gonna miss you, girl," he mumbled as Darcy turned the corner and disappeared. "You and everything else."

Just weeks ago, his parents had informed him that they were moving the family to Detroit to live with Uncle James and Aunt Lorraine. The news struck Hakeem like a bomb blast, turning his world upside down overnight. Yet, as bad as it was, the announcement wasn't the worst thing he heard recently.

Five months ago, his father was diagnosed with kidney cancer. Surgery, chemotherapy, and the sickness it caused had reduced Dad's strength so much that he could no longer perform his job as a warehouse manager. For three months, Hakeem watched as his father's size diminished and his face aged. Though the treatment had stopped the disease, it left Dad a shadow of his former self, and it devastated the family's savings.

"We've spent everything we had on medical bills, baby," Mom said tearfully a few weeks ago. "I don't know what's gonna happen. But no matter what, I need you to be strong, Hakeem. I need you to be the man around here."

Hakeem nodded solemnly in response, expecting that the family would find a small apartment nearby. He was even ready to share a bedroom with his seven-year-old twin sisters so his parents could save money. But Hakeem never imagined that his Uncle James would invite the family to Detroit or that Dad would agree to go.

"I don't know what choice we have," Hakeem's father explained when he told the family the news. "Even though the cancer's stopped, the doctors say it could be months before I get my strength back. And without our savings, we can't afford to stay here any more," he said, massaging his forehead, his scratchy voice sounding much older than his forty years. "I wish I didn't have to do this to you. I'm sorry."

"Don't worry, Dad. It'll be all right," Hakeem had replied, half believing his words. Besides their money problems, Hakeem knew there was always a chance the cancer could return, a possibility which kept him up many nights, his heart racing with fear. In a few days, Dad would meet with doctors in Detroit to see if the cancer was still in remission.

Even though no one admitted it, Hakeem knew one reason Dad was moving them to Detroit was to keep his family together in case his health took a turn for the worse.

Watching the movers load his family's belongings into the storage truck, Hakeem felt as he had years earlier when someone robbed his church. The stolen money had been collected for a little girl who had leukemia, but that didn't stop the thieves from taking every cent. He had decided then that life was cruel. His father's cancer diagnosis, his horrific battle with the disease, and the sudden move were just the latest proof.

"You all right, Hakeem?" Dad asked, snapping Hakeem from his thoughts. "I know it isn't easy sayin' goodbye to your friends, especially Darcy."

"I'm fine, Dad. Darcy and I said what we had to say," Hakeem replied, trying to hide his sadness. *Be strong*, he reminded himself.

"That's it," his mother said as the movers closed the back of the truck. "Everything's packed, and the airport taxi is here. We gotta leave now. Come on, everyone."

Hakeem grabbed his suitcase, the

notebook he used as a journal, and his old guitar, and took one last look at his house. Without furniture and pictures, it was a cold and empty shell, not the place where he grew up.

I can't believe I'm not coming back, he thought, glancing down the street toward his school, Bluford High, just a few blocks away.

I need you to be the man around here, his mother's words echoed in his mind.

"Come on, son," his father urged. The family was waiting in the cab.

Hakeem took a deep breath, wiped his eyes, and said a silent goodbye to his world.

Good men beat down
Smiles turn to frowns
There is no logic
In a world so tragic

Hakeem read the words from his notebook. He had written them when his father first mentioned the move to Detroit. It seemed as if years had passed, not weeks. He flipped the page bitterly.

The dull hum of the plane's engines had lulled the rest of his family to sleep, but Hakeem could not relax. His mind swirled with thoughts of Darcy and his closest friends, Cooper and Tarah.

Maybe one day he'd write a song for them, he thought. Hakeem turned to a blank sheet of paper and stared at the tiny blue lines on the page. For years, he'd been singing and playing his guitar. He joined his church choir in second grade. Later, when he developed a stuttering problem in middle school, he discovered that it disappeared whenever he sang. Years ago, Mr. Smalley, the choir director, praised his voice.

"God gave you some talents, young man. Be sure you use them."

Hakeem hadn't sung for the church in years. But he did perform from time to time at Bluford. Even when he wasn't singing, he was always jotting lyrics in his notebook for songs he might sing one day. Music and writing were two things he relied on when the rest of the world was a mess. In his songs, he could control everything. There was no cancer. No goodbyes. Not unless he decided it.

Hakeem glanced at the notebook and tried to remember everything he knew about Detroit. He'd been there once before. It was ten years ago, when he was just six years old. Then, his father was to him the strongest person in the world. A person immune to disease, to cancer and chemotherapy. A superhero.

What Hakeem did most during the visit was eat huge dinners at his aunt and uncle's house and play video games with his cousin Savon. The two boys were nearly the same age, though Savon was much heavier.

"Savon's a husky boy," his mother used to say.

During the weeks he stayed in Detroit, Hakeem and Savon played for hours on end. Hakeem remembered once the two were playing catch in the street when some teens stole their ball.

"Thanks, Wimpy and Blimpy," the teens mocked as they strolled down the street, passing the ball around. The moment had stuck in Hakeem's mind. The teasing hurt, but it had also made him feel close to his cousin. They shared a special bond that moment. They were family.

But when Hakeem returned to California, he gradually lost touch with Savon. An awkward phone conversation three years ago at Christmas was the last time they talked. And now, after so many years, the dim memory of Detroit was bittersweet, a reminder of a past long gone.

Staring out of the small window next to his seat, Hakeem watched a veil of wispy clouds pass beneath him. His memories did little to erase the hole the move was carving into his life.

I miss home already, he thought, stretching back in his seat and closing his eyes.

I miss home.

"Are we there yet? Are we at Uncle James's house?" asked Charlene, one of Hakeem's younger twin sisters.

"Almost," Dad said wearily from the passenger seat of the rental car. Since Dad got sick, Mom drove the family everywhere.

"You've been asking that ever since we landed," snapped Charmaine, rolling her eyes at her sister. "Can't you just stop talking?"

Hakeem yawned and said nothing. The hour wait to get off the plane and pick up their bags was tiring. Now, the twenty-five minute drive through city traffic to Uncle James's house felt like slow torture. His sisters only made it worse.

"Is this it?" Charlene asked suddenly as the car stopped at a traffic light. "Is this where we're going to live at?"

"Shut up," Charmaine groaned.

"Girls!" Mom snapped. "If you don't stop whining, I'm gonna give you both somethin' to whine about."

"Make a right up there on Sawyer Street," Dad interrupted. His tired voice silenced everyone.

Outside, the houses were older and more densely packed than those back home. Made of red brick, many were row homes, though a few bigger houses did stand alone on some blocks. At the end of one street, Hakeem spotted a playground with a swing set and basketball court. A steel fence surrounded the park, making it look more like a prison yard than a playground.

Several teenage boys were shooting baskets as Hakeem and his family passed. One reminded Hakeem of his best friend, Cooper Hodden. Coop was one of the toughest people he knew, but he was also one of the nicest. When he found out that Hakeem was moving away, Coop had almost cried.

"Stay with *us*, Hak! My mom says we

got room for you," he insisted. "Besides, she likes you more than she likes me."

For a second, Hakeem had considered Cooper's offer. He desperately wanted to stay, but he couldn't abandon his family. Not with everyone depending on him. Still, as he gazed out at the unfamiliar neighborhood, part of him wished he'd listened to Coop.

On a corner up ahead, Hakeem noticed two guys sitting on the steps of a house. One had a sharp angular face and wore a sideways baseball cap. The other was shaved bald and shirtless, his chest as wide as a barrel. Both glared at the car as the family approached.

Hakeem felt a nervous twinge in the pit of his stomach. Seeming to sense tension, Hakeem's mother pushed the accelerator, and the rented sedan lurched forward.

Welcome to the neighborhood, Hakeem thought bitterly to himself.

Excerpt copyright © 2004 by Townsend Press, Inc.

THEY'VE GROWN APART.

Can they still get along?

Hakeem and Savon have nothing in common anymore. But when circumstances force the cousins to live together, will they be able to put aside their differences?

SCHOLASTIC

www.scholastic.com

BLUFORD8

SCHOLASTIC and associated logos are trademarks and/or registered trademarks of Scholastic Inc.